812116

Naomi Mitchison

IMAGES OF AFRICA

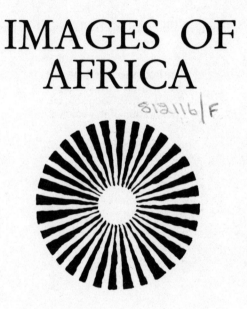

812116/F

CANONGATE
Edinburgh
1980

First Published in 1980
by Canongate Publishing Ltd
17 Jeffrey Street, Edinburgh
Scotland

© Naomi Mitchison 1980

ISBN 0 903937 70 0

Design and Illustrations by James Hutcheson

The Publishers acknowledge
the financial assistance of the
Scottish Arts Council in the
publication of this volume

Typeset in 11/13pt. Garamond by
Hewer Text Composition Services

Printed and bound in Great Britain by
Billing and Sons Ltd, Guildford, London and Worcester

FOREWORD

I have to make it clear, not least to myself, what I have been trying to do in this book. Serious authors are always attempting to build bridges which will allow communication where none existed before or where it had gone wrong. To my mind, much of the communication between Europe and Africa is either superficial or has been deflected by a clash of values. I have therefore tried to build bridges of understanding with those parts of Africa with which I have been in sympathetic contact. The stories try to establish this kind of contact, not between reason and reason, not in terms of economics or politics, but in the deeper level of the imagination. If this bridge can be crossed, others may be built.

Some of these stories have borrowings, both from stories I heard or half heard in the Kgatleng, or from friends of the Bushmen. Some are based on actual happenings or imagined happenings of today, in Botswana, Zambia and the west coast. Some have passed the test of reading aloud and being told that, yes, you have got it right, or even Yes, how did you know? I hope they will help towards a mutual understanding which is deeply needed.

CONTENTS

Images of Botswana

In summer the goats eat the marula fruits from under the trees; in winter the boys gather the stones from the goat kraals and crack them for their kernels. One marula stone is thrown by a little boy at another; it misses him and falls between two rocks. It has been through the dark, stinking body of the goat; it has been seized on by the boy; it has escaped. It grows into a beautiful tree.

Listen to the sound of the stars. Listen with your outer ear and then with your inner ear. They travel very far away. Without our seeing their places change. Ourselves singing round the beer drink, we cannot hear the sound of the stars. Cradle of lightnings, sing to us a song for dreaming true. We, your children, listen. The sun's sound is the heat striking the dust, the light striking the red, eye-hurting flower, the long day goldening the skin. What shall we get out of the sky sounds? In what basket can we cage them? What bird will sing them to us?

The rain hunts over our roofs, soft on the thatch, with hard hoofs on tin. Then it is away. Come back, even with thunder, even with lightning. Without you we cannot grow; we are killed. The earth hardens and longs and dies. Oh rain, rain, come, hunt us.

In my dream I was my father. Or did my father dream me, so that I am my father's dream? And she answered: In my dream I was my mother. If my mother dreamed me, she must have also have dreamed you, since now we are one.

1

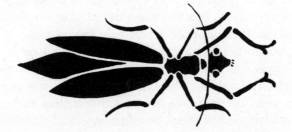

There Here Then Now

There was sand and grass and bushes; there were flat-topped trees and a very blue very wide sky and a hot sun. There was this animal grazing and Kara Tuma crept up carefully, carefully, stopping and becoming a bush or an ant-hill or a shadow, and still the animal did not shift or scrape with its hoof or lift up the horns on its head from where its mouth was down grazing. But what was it? Could it be a buffalo? No, for its horns came from wide apart on a mild forehead. No, for it was somehow a different shape. But it was meat. It raised its head and looked at him with large eyes. And Kara Tuma drew his bow and shot it right through the eye into the brain. So the animal died and it was much meat.

Now Kara Tuma was a yellowish brown man, not tall, but he had a friend who was dark brown and altogether bigger, indeed this friend was his cousin. Their grandfather long ago had three sons. The eldest son by his first wife was Kara Tuma's father; his second son by his second wife was the father of the brown man, who was called Lentswe, which meant that he was hard like a stone but supple like a word. But his third son by his third wife had been pale and sickly in looks and liked to keep in the shade of bushes and by and by he had gone to a cooler place at the back of the

3

north wind and the rest of the family lost all trace of him. Because of his paleness they called him Whiteskin, which was not very kind, because when the sun came on his arms and face he became quite a nice pale brown and his hair, which was rather long, was about the same colour as Kara Tuma's skin. But the other two never thought about him.

However, Lentswe, the brown man who was big and strong, used often to see his cousin and they exchanged things which pleased them, or asked one another questions. So now, Kara Tuma called out to Lentswe, "I have much meat here, come and eat!" But when Lentswe saw the animal he frowned and said, "But this is a cow. That was why the animal did not run away. You should not have killed her."

"Oh, I am sad!" said Kara Tuma. "But I will tell you when I see another."

So in a while Kara Tuma saw another of these animals and instead of shooting it he ran to tell his cousin Lentswe. Then Lentswe came softly and put his hand on the cow and stroked her and at last his hand went down to her udder and began to pull at the teats. But the cow went on chewing. Lentswe had a pot with him and he milked the cow into the pot. "Now there is a pot of beautiful milk," he said. "Let us drink it."

But Kara Tuma had never so much as sipped a cow's milk and he was afraid to taste it, seeing it had come hot out of a cow. "No," he said, "you must drink it, my cousin, and I will just lick the inside of the pot." Oh how foolish he was, for that was what he did, and that was how things went on between the dark brown people and the yellow brown people! After that the dark brown man made a kraal out of branches; whenever he found a cow he drove her in; soon he had many calves and some of them were bull calves. But when they skinned the cow which had been killed, Lentswe kept the long thongs, because he would need them for his cows and only gave Kara Tuma pieces of string. But Kara Tuma used the string very cleverly to make all kinds of snares for the small animals and birds that live among the bushes and in the tall grass.

Another time again, Kara Tuma found some grass with a heavy head on top of it. He bit off some of this, but the husks scratched his mouth, so he decided to burn it all down. But along came his cousin Lentswe and said, "That is another foolish thing you have done! This is grain and it must be gathered and pounded and then we shall have porridge." But Kara Tuma did not want to help pick the heads which had not been burned and which were a little prickly and he did not like porridge. But Lentswe had porridge with milk and sometimes with sour milk, which was even nicer than sweet milk, and he grew fat, and so did his wives and children, and by and by he found that when there was enough porridge he could also make beer. But Kara Tuma made another and stronger kind of drink out of roots which grew wild, so he was not interested in the beer.

However things went well for a while, or at least not ill, though Kara Tuma and Lentswe did not see so much of one another because Lentswe was busy teaching his cows to pull sledges and ploughs, and growing better crops of corn as well as other kinds of food, and Kara Tuma was snaring and hunting, and when he had time he would draw the animals he wanted to see on the inside rocks of great caves. And his wives were busy finding new kinds of roots and collecting seeds and fruits. But both of them took time for singing and dancing and whatever happiness was floating around.

Then along came their cousin whom they had never seen, the son of the pale one who did not like the sun, and he was even whiter, so that he had to wear clothes all over himself so as to keep the sun entirely away. However he was their cousin and went around with them and by and by they found a great thing made of metal with pieces sticking out from it here and there, and some were round and turned by themselves and it made a noise like no beast they knew. "We must stop this," said Lentswe.

5

"Yes, indeed, let us kill it," said Kara Tuma, and notched in an arrow. "Where do you think is its heart, Cousin Lentswe?"

But the pale man said, "You are fools, both of you! It is an engine. It will do things for you. It has strength. And it has a brother who will carry you about even as far as the back of the north wind where I come from. It will even kill for you."

"What does it eat?" said Lentswe, but he kept his spear in his hand. He was not sure.

"It will eat half your crops and half your beasts and as for you, Cousin Kara Tuma, you will have to give it the skin of every animal you kill. It will want every elephant tusk and every leopardskin. I am sorry, but this is necessary; it is called progress. That is a new word. But think what it will do for us! I shall of course be the one to guide it because I know its ways, and perhaps, my dear Cousins, you yourselves will have to work to keep up with this splendid engine or machine, which will do so much for all of us."

So Lentswe and Kara Tuma looked at one another, and looked at the chugging quivering machine. Kara Tuma said nothing, but shook his head, and Lentswe said, "Truly, Cousin Whiteskin, we are not much interested; you may keep this machine and we hope it will not hurt you, for it looks fiercer than a charging buffalo." So they went away and left the younger cousin Whiteskin with the machine, and he guided it and its brothers into doing many kinds of things which went well for Whiteskin, but less well for Lentswe and still less well for Kara Tuma. All that they knew and did became altered and looked less good and there was less dancing and singing and the machines had to be fed. So they began to blame one another, and above all to blame and hate Cousin Whiteskin and these hard powerful machines of his. And just as the cleverness and will to live in difficult places went from the small desert animals into Kara Tuma, and just as the strength and goodness of the cows went into Lentswe, so did the fierceness and unlife of the

7

machine go into Whiteskin. But this was not something that any of the cousins understood.

Now their great-great-grandfather who seldom took much notice, since he was occupied with better and more interesting events, decided that here was a bad situation and he must take a look at it. So back he came; he was a Mantis. In fact he seldom took human form; that would have been awkward, for whose particular form would it be? If he became a lion or a leopard it could easily have been alarming to those who did not recognise him. If he had been a bird or an antelope they could have killed him. But indeed it would be incorrect to speak of him as a male person; he was also their great-great-grandmother, food provider and inventor, and fountain of kindness. It would have been useless for him not also to be her.

So first the green Mantis leapt upon the machine, which recognised him and stopped in his honour. Nor could his child, Whiteskin, in any way make it start, since it had recognised a greater power. And then he showed himself to the cows of his child Lentswe, and at once they broke out of their kraal, as though the walls were made of thin grass, and began to eat the crops, and neither Lentswe nor his wives could in any way stop this going on. And finally he went to visit his child Kara Tuma, who at once recognised him, since the Mantis is well known in those places where Kara Tuma hunts and snares, and his wives dig for roots. "I see you well, great-great-grandfather," he said. "I am altogether happy to greet you."

Mantis twisted and nodded his green head in recognition and scratched his long neck with one leg. "Now my children are all equal," he said, "but perhaps my child Kara Tuma is the best off, because he is so clever with that piece of string. Should we now start fresh, my children? I ask you all." For the other two had followed and they knew their great-great-grandfather, though they did not care for the knowledge, since it seemed greater than all the other kinds of knowledge

8

they had and was, because of that, unwelcome. Mantis understood this, but he did not choose to make himself more acceptable and he could see thoughts and suspicions boiling and bubbling like porridge or beer. "You will stop thinking dirty thoughts about one another and about me, my children," he said. "And instead you must remember that an equal handful of life has gone to each one of you."

Now at that Lentswe and Whiteskin looked at one another and Whiteskin whispered, "If my machine will work again, shall we share it?" And Lentswe said, "If I can drive my cows back, would you like some fresh milk, for it is better than that stuff you get out of a tin?" But neither of them spoke to Kara Tuma because he had this yellow brown skin that seemed strange to them, and because he was smaller than either of them, but above all, because it was clear that he knew Mantis in a way that they did not, since many other shapes came between Mantis and them.

But Mantis came and went and fleetingly he was a lion, or a thunderstorm, or hunger and fear itself. But Kara Tuma stood holding his bow and his bare toes gripped into the ground and it seemed to them that the thing he held was life and death and that the earth flowered through him. So there they are, looking with changing minds, and Mantis, their great-great-grandfather, is watching them.

9

The Hill Behind
for Seingwaeng

In the Valley without Water they cried for rain. Oh let it rain, rain, a soft and comforting day-long rain like a girl's skin, the skin of her face, her neck, her breasts that would some day sweeten into milk, the long smooth skin of her thighs. Wet rain. Without rain they died a little every day. The small children died first, not playing, going slack on their mother's knees. But also the big men who wanted to be ploughing, they died partly. They sat in the shade, not speaking, their hands and heads drooping over their knees. Heat hit them out of the dust, their toes curled up like dry leaves. The herd boys took the cattle further and further to drink, but they might go three, four days without water. Some of them lay down and died. A man's pride, a man's riches, fell day by day as though one threw gold into a bottomless crack in the ground. Even if the cattle died beside paths it was no use to skin them; there was no meat on their bones. The women walked many miles to carry water from the wells which still held a little deep down. When they came back, weary, they could have drunk the whole pot themselves, but it was for their men and their children.

Out beyond the Valley it was worse. In dry miles of sand and thorny bushes Tsaxau uncovered the nest his mother had made and took out one ostrich shell full of water. One egg of water is not much for a family, but his mother and grandmother had both died; they had become too tired to move their legs on; they had been left in the shelter. Nobody would come back for them, ever. It was so. Always it had been so. He thought of his mother when he lifted out the egg of water. Tsaxau gave some to his little brother, but most to his father. His father might kill something. When he had drunk the water his father prayed that he might find something to kill.

The people of the Valley without Water went to their King. "Make rain!" they said, "we need rain. Our cattle die. Let there be rain, Kgosi, call on all the Kings so that through them you may speak for us to God."

Kgosi answered them, "I hear you, people. But my cattle too are dying. The sky is unkind. The smell of rain is far. I have tried to speak for you, but it is useless."

They began to mock him. The women beat him with branches. They brought a black ox and stayed silently watching, in case he was moved to sacrifice and open a way to the ancestors and through them to God.

He went away from his people. He went into his house. It was not the large, goldenly-thatched round of his wife of the first house, which had many pleasant things in it, cooking pots and sieves, fine leather skirts and necklaces of beads and gold, blankets and soft furs, and over all a smell of women that would stir like a snake in a man. He did not go to the houses of any of his wives, although they stood in the doorways watching. One had been pounding grain. Another was plastering a piece of her wall which had broken. She used even water from far off for this, but a King's wife, although she is not the great wife, should have all things seemly round her. He had married them for many reasons of family-binding and an ending of old quarrels; he had given them much pleasure. There were small children. As they looked his way, eyes glowed or were cast down. They would have given him what water they had, although they too had little. But he went past them to his own house and sat there in stillness and darkness.

For indeed he had done all that should have been done for the Valley without Water. He had made the *tshitlho* for rain, using the herbs which had been shown him and told him, and also parts of water-beasts and birds, the frog and the fish-eagle, whose wings are like thunder-clouds. He had secretly sent to the roads out, and laid the sticks and beaten the earth in case some sorcerer from another place had laid a curse and stopped the rain from coming. Early, before first light, he had sent children with new, small pots to sprinkle the lands with water into which the *tshitlho* had been stirred. And he himself had strained and sweated in hard prayer, knowing that to be a King is nothing if he cannot help his people.

So now he thought there was perhaps one more thing to do. He slept alone and his dreams could be made clear either one way or the other. Very early in the morning he sent for the Princess Naledi, the star. Now stars can be bright and lead people to their homes, or they can be darkened by clouds and shifting in the sky, and so it was with Naledi. She did not wish to come when she was sent for nor yet to understand what was asked of her. She looked away from her father; her toes scuffled at a small crack in the floor, her fingers twisted her beads. Her father became angry, but a King must hold his anger in, even as he must hold his pain. Yet it became as though his words were a whip striking her and her eyes went dark and she held her head up and at last she listened. She was afraid but also not afraid, since it was something new. Her father saw this on her. "Come," he said, and walked out of his house, she following.

Now all this while Tsaxau's father and Tsaxau himself were looking for a thing to kill, since hunger was at them all and the small one cried almost all the time. They left him and went hunting, silently. They looked also for the wild melon

13

which is a little bitter, but full of almost water. Far off across dry grass and thin bushes they saw ostriches, and now they separated and ran like shadows, each with his bow. Tsaxau ran faster than his father, but he had not spent so many years sighting and thinking along the flight of the small arrow with death smeared on its tip.

A beast slipped through the rustle of grass ahead of Tsaxau, but it was not a beast one could eat; it was a beast of sharp claws and tearing teeth, though a small one; its flesh was not good for a man. Tsaxau did not bend his bow, but as he came nearer to the ostriches that was what he did. The male ostrich was very big; he was taller than two men. His wives must obey him and run when he called to them. This was the one his father would shoot. And as he thought that, the arrow of his father came through the air. But the ostrich had jumped and the arrow hid itself in his thick tail feathers without touching his skin. Yet the ostrich was disturbed and started to run with his great naked legs, calling to his wives. There was only one shot for Tsaxau, who was now also running. This was a female, not very big, she had become confused. He shot her. She ran for a little, then lay down.

Now they were pulling out her feathers. Before, it had been his mother who had done this and Tsaxau cried without making any noise, because he thought of her so much that she seemed to be there, but when he turned his head she was not. He and his father did not do this so well as his mother and grandmother had done; the feathers stuck to their hands and they shook their hands about. Inside the ostrich were eggs which were tender to eat; he would keep one for his little brother. About and about the feathers flew. The wind caught them.

The people of the Valley without Water watched the King and the Princess walking through the dust, past the shadow of the high dark branches under which the counsellors and elders sat and where there had been good talk and grave laughter and the coolness of water or beer. But now the heat beat through it. Some, seeing Naledi wearing the beaded kilt half way to her knees and the necklaces and bracelets which were her due, shook their heads. "She is wilful," they said, "she will not do what Kgosi tells her." For some of them had guessed what it might be.

"She should have been beaten," they said, "even as a child she wanted too much."

"She is not beautiful," said another, "she is like a boy." And they spoke of the way she held her head in the air, so that the golden earrings bobbed in her ears, instead of keeping her eyes cast down and her smile unseen. She had slapped the hand of a boy who had gently touched her on an evening of dance; it had been a hard slap; he was her cousin. It could have been suitable to let his hand rest for a moment. At the time of her marriage there would be feasting for all the people of the Valley without Water. Fat beasts would be killed; there would be meat and beer and porridge in the great pots.

But the King and the Princess walked away without greetings, only the small click of the tongue from one or another. He carried his gun, which was a muzzle-loader with a date inlaid with brass on the stock, and also two spears. He had a cloak of soft fur slung over his shoulder. Naledi carried the bag of powder and the bullets, and also a small bag with water and a handful of meal in a little cooking pot. They walked out beyond the sad unploughed lands, the hard, sun-baked earth where only a few thorns showed, breaking through. It was hot, hot. The dry land breathed nothing but scorching hotness at them.

A certain hill had seemed in the dawn a violet shadow. Now it was near and steep with great rocks piled and poised and trees and bushes growing between, which seemed greener and more full of leaves than the bushes at home. It was a hill that the King knew and that the Princess had heard many stories about: a hill of ancient stories that was called the Hill Behind. And it seemed to Naledi that she was beginning to know what was laid on her to do. They stood under a tall tree and the King looked carefully at his young daughter. He thought, Yes, she is a brave one, and she will need to be. He said to her, "We have finished the journey on plain ground; our feet are dusty. Now, for you, my daughter, begins the magic journey."

She laid down the bag of powder and the bullets and looked at him and asked, "Shall I come back from it, my father?"

He said, "If you are brave and clever you will come back. If you are worthy of the ancestors. I will wait for you a night and a day." She seemed to straighten herself. "And another night," he suddenly said; and then, "You will pass to the great clefted rock and there leave your clothes and your necklaces: everything on arms and legs and ears. Then you must climb."

"May I take your spear, my father?"

"No," he said, "but you will not need it. You will see wild beasts. You will see many small snakes. Do not fear them, above all do not hurt any of these small snakes. They will be there to strengthen you. This you will feel in yourself."

"To strengthen me for what, my father?"

"At the end, at the very end, behind everything, behind the rising of the moon, you will meet the rain-snake, Kgwanyape." Now it was said. He watched her take a deep breath and her breasts, which were still so small, quivered; the shining beads moved on her soft skin.

"And then?"

"Truly, I do not know. This is something very old. It is from the ancestors. But you will be strong. You are a princess, my daughter. Do not fight the rain-snake. Even if he is also the terrible storm-wind. This is all I know." And he stood there and saw her walk to the split rock and in the last light take off all she was wearing and climb naked up and over the split in the hard, towering rock. And the moon was not yet risen.

Naledi began the magic climb. She looked up at the sky. Was she, too, a star? One of the big stars low down that seemed to change colour, or one of the high, quiet, small stars which stay in their patterns and together make the starlight in which she could see this and that? There seemed to be a very small and narrow path between the rocks, although here and there a thorn bush had grown out across it and tried to catch her. She felt a little trickle of blood down one arm. She saw a small, thin snake and stopped; but she did not pick up a stick or stone to hurt it, and it slipped away. And then she moved and laid her foot on the little twisting spoor of the snake, and she felt a kind of strengthening beginning. There were noises all round, night noises and smells with them, which she could not quite name. Was this the place of leopards? She made up her mind that she was one of the big stars. How can a leopard leap at a star?

And now the moon was rising, very large, golden turning to silver. It seemed she was walking across a shoulder of the hill which one did not see from below, a kind of platform of worn and flattened rock, and here indeed were beasts of the night. One with a sloping back, dog legs and shining eyes, passed her, and other shadows, big or small, slipped from rock to rock. There were snuffles and cries and breathings. But especially there were small snakes, and these she did not touch to harm them. Once she heard far below her a lion roaring and then she found herself afraid for her father, and this was strange. She was not afraid for herself and before this she had not felt love for her father; until now they had shared nothing. But now she was sharing with him in the deepest need of the people and she knew far down in her heart that he now felt love for her and his spirit would have tried to be with her on the magic journey which yet she must do alone.

And then in the moonlight she saw that there were hollows in the flat rock bed and that these reflected the

18

moon. Water. Hollows, deep pools, of water. How? She
went to one and knelt by it, seeing her own quivering
moonlit reflection. She dipped in her hand, her wrist, her
arm. It was deep, deep. She felt something twining and
when she lifted her arm there was a small, shining water-
snake which slipped off her and back into the pool. She
stood up with her body wetted from her cupped hand.
There was a tree growing, and as she passed it many large
moths came and sipped from her damp skin. They were
beautiful, with markings of grey and brown and silver. She
brushed them away gently, moving along and always up
between the dark pools. All belonged to the Hill Behind.
Then something larger than a moth came circling round her;
it did not seem right to her, it was alive. She brushed at it
more sharply and it fell into a pool of water. As it fell she
seemed for a moment to hear a voice inside her head, calling
"Mother". Yet although she understood this, it was yet not
a known word but perhaps only a thought loosened from
her mind. The thing was swallowed by the dark water. It
had travelled far, whirling on the winds, up and down and
up. It was a feather from the she-ostrich. It had blood on it.

The moon was high now, above the crest of the hill. As
she walked, she began to feel sleep coming on her in short
waves, so that between one tree and the next, although her
legs carried her, it was as though she had lived through a
whole life. Once she leant against a rock and it seemed to
melt and take her into soft darkness, but in only a few
breaths she was awake again. She watched the shadows of
her own moving body, moon shadows darker than sun
shadows. But she could see colours; here and there were
very small flowers, blue or yellow. Flowers of the Hill.
Their roots must have known water.

Now she was coming up on to the moonlit crest above the
shadows, and dawn was nowhere. Then Kgwanyape, the
rain-snake, was beside her, was mounting her, coil upon
coil, throwing weight here or there until she staggered on

her feet but yet he held her up and his pointed snake face
with its bright cold eyes looked into her face and his forked
and strange tongue that had licked her body all over in his
climbing now flicked into her ears, her nostrils, her eyes and
her mouth, bringing a sweet darkness and the thought of
rain.

In that sweet dark of dreams many lives happened to
Naledi. She was a warrior, a leader of men; she was a horse
galloping, all four hooves ringing on the ground; she was a
fish slithering among white roots and green weeds; she was
an eagle quartering the land, guarding, guarding: and again
she was a water-creature, a dragonfly with all-coloured
wings skimming and touching. So that when she awoke it
was no surprise that she felt drops of water on her skin. And
now the morning star had risen. There was no moon but it
was time to go down the hill, to go down with rain.

It was easier going down. When she passed the shoulder
of flat rocks it was beginning to be dawn and she could see
that the great holes were now brimming over and flowing
together into twists and trickles of water. The rain was not
cold, nor yet dusty; it had not come with a harsh wind, but
straight from the clouds. As it grew light she went more
quickly and came to the clefted rock. There was her kilt and
there her necklaces and earrings, her bracelets and leg
ornaments, all a little damp. Cool, cool the morning, and
looking across, there was her father, his head on his knees,
his spears beside him, the gun under a fold of his cloak, and,
when she was dressed she came running and calling through
the beautiful rain and everywhere there were soft grey
clouds bending low over the land and from the rocks and
stones of the Hill Behind small springs bubbling and
twisting with clear water.

Her father lifted his head. He stood. He saw her. He came
towards her and there was great happiness. "Greetings, my
daughter," he said. "I see you. I see you with rain!"

"I come with rain," she said, and now she was a little cold, but he put round her the half of the cloak which was warm from his own body. Then both of them drank from a small new pool under the rocks.

"When you did not come in the morning I was terribly afraid for you," he said.

"But I came in the morning," she answered.

"Not the morning after the evening when you began the magic journey." At this she fell quiet and she thought of Kgwanyape, the rain-snake, in the night and the snake eyes like shining stones and the licking fork of the tongue and all that had happened in her long dreams. "So you met the snake in the end," he said. "You met Kgwanyape and you were brave. And he gave you rain. Through you I have rain. Through you, my daughter, the people have rain. We shall be saved alive."

She said, "That is good, my father. But tell me a certain thing. I heard lions roaring, and I was afraid for you. But all was well?"

"There was roaring," he said, "but, as I caught up my spears it was for you I was afraid, you naked and alone." And then both of them laughed a little. He said, "You are somewhat changed, Naledi my daughter, star of the people."

"And you too," she said, "my father." And then she busied herself with making a fire where the rain had not yet come through the thick branches of a tree, and on this she put the small pot with the meal and water from the new, fresh pool. While she had been on her magic journey he had not eaten. It was well, and in a while they shared the porridge, while the rain began to come in big, pleasing drops through their roof of branches.

The King and his daughter walked back in the light soft rain. The ground was no longer hard and scorching under their feet. Here and there long brown pools were gathering. Soon, soon the grass would come. When they came through the lands and nearer the people, it was seen that such oxen as were fit for ploughing were being taken to the wagons and sledges, on to which already the ploughs had been loaded. As soon as the people saw Kgosi coming, and his daughter alive at his side, they rushed to greet them with words and songs, and the women shrilled at the backs of their throats, and all at once it was said that the Princess Naledi was indeed beautiful.

High up on the magic hill the ostrich feather was drinking life out of the pool. It was drawing to itself the features of an ostrich, a she-ostrich asleep and still small.

In the desert, Tsaxau and his father and his little brother chewed at the tough ostrich-meat. It had been partly roasted over the fire, and there was a little salt, also Tsaxau had found a root that could be eaten. They wished it had been meat of buck or wild pig. Yet it was food. And then a small dark cloud came over them and it split with a roar of rain. Tsaxau filled again the ostrich-shell from the hidden nest and other rain was caught in melon rinds and the meat went down better. But Tsaxau still thought of his mother.

So it was that the people of the Valley without Water were saved. For a time, even, the stream that ran through the valley once and that had seemed to be dead, began to run again, pleasant to the feet. The grass came and the cattle ate and the flesh came back on their ribs and hip bones and knotty backbones. There was ploughing. There was milk. For a time death would keep away. And for a time Naledi was quiet at her mother's house, or else she was making songs. Her small breasts grew; her bracelets and leg-bands looked well on firm flesh. She went away out of the Valley for the raising of her *mophato*, the time of learning how to be altogether a woman. But of what had happened on the Hill Behind she did not speak, either at home or to those of the older *mophato* who cared for her and taught her and sometimes for her own good hurt her a little in the lessons of becoming a woman, one of the generations of women of the people.

Then came uncles of young men asking for her in marriage, and her father sent for her. "I will make no answer that you would not wish," he said, "for you are the lintel of the door of my house and there is yet much which you must know and which, later, even when you are old, you will use to help our people. Yet it may be that your eyes have seen that there is a young man or an older man with whom a branch might be bent or a cooking-pot brought to boil. And although an order comes to the eyes to shut themselves, yet a small bird takes a message to the heart."

So, after a while, Naledi said in a low voice, "There is such a one. Indeed, his younger uncle has a well-known and beautifully-spotted ox which my father has seen." She looked away and then she spoke again. "But I do not know if I can be given. Kgwanyape also is my uncle and the elder brother of my father's fathers."

So the King called together those of his people who were skilled in such matters, and they came to his house halfway between midnight and noon and consulted the *ditaola* and spoke long, both with the ancestors and among themselves. One of them had been chosen to snuff smoke and to drink the *tshitlho* which had been prepared, and so he was able to see and speak with Kgwanyape, although in a body of shadows and not as he had been on the magic hill. After this they told Kgosi that the rain-snake would not come between the Princess and her need. But also they could see something else, which troubled them, which appeared always in the *ditaola*, some question of which the answer was not plain, and they did not know what it could be, only that it was on its way. But the King was glad that the rain-snake would give Naledi to be a wife and he hoped she would have as many children as there are stars in the sky. So there was betrothal and a great brewing and cooking and singing, and the many beads which Naledi wore were like a garment of flowers on a rained-upon field before the ploughing.

But the night after the betrothal when by custom certain

things are allowed, late, late, when all others were sleeping, Naledi lay on her mat at the side of her mother's house where one that was welcome could creep in along the wall, stooping, and find her. From far off there was still a singing of the people which became part of her and her body became full of hope. Then there was a rustling and a shape in the doorway. But it was not the shape of the one she waited for and it seemed to have a long neck and long legs and it was not a person at all and she, who had not been afraid on the magic climb, now screamed for fear. It went away. But all in the house had wakened and the one who had been waiting and who had been waited for, did not come.

Now this thing went on, and not only for Naledi. The comrades of the one to whom she had been betrothed spoke in jests and riddles and he answered angrily, for truly he had come, but instead of what he hoped for, a spirit with a long neck had stood in the doorway. And at last his uncle came to the younger brother of the King and asked how it was that the full gourd was taken from the lips and the honey was locked in the tree-trunk and the night-ostrich stood in the door of the house? Now this was reported to the King, for indeed the thing was most strange, and he sent for Naledi to ask what she had done, and she came in tears and distress, saying that it was so indeed and no fault of hers, and what could be done?

Now it was thought at first that this could be a sorcery which had been put there by some jealous or angry person, and all that could be done was done, so that this sorcery should turn back on the head of the one who had put it there. But still the night-ostrich came and it seemed to grow larger and plainer. Now even in the daytime Naledi would look fearfully over her shoulder and catch a glimpse of it. Sometimes too her comrades of the *mophato* saw it fleetingly, so that they were doubled up with sickness. And the one to whom she was betrothed became more angry in himself and felt that it was her doing or her father's doing, and perhaps there would be the same or another curse on her wedding, which should be soon with the first new rains. Fear mixed with the anger, for this was nothing he could fight. So Naledi sent for the wise men to say that something, anything, must be done, and they in turn spoke to the King. The thing they wanted to do did not please him. But it was so, that all was becoming worse and hard words said, and Kgosi felt the anger of the family of the betrothed as something which might hurt all his people. So at last he said Yes, they had his leave to do it.

In this way certain men from the Valley went out carrying leather cords and in the evening they came back with what they had caught. It was a young boy of the outer people, the small ones, the yellow-faced whose speech is not ours. It was Tsaxau. He had run from them, but they had made a trap as though he was a beast, and now like a beast they would treat him. In the great kraal there was a sharpening of knives and with it laughter that had a cruel edge like a knife.

The Princess Naledi had been with other girls pounding grain and singing, hoping not to see the ostrich. She looked round and there it was, nearer than ever and more like a real ostrich and less like something in her mind. It flapped its wings, it hissed through its beak and it drove her, and now she ran from it trying to escape, but always it was there. By now the ostrich had become entirely solid, a day-ostrich, and many people saw it and some tried to come between it and the Princess, but it was no use. She ran and screamed, dodging between the houses, in and out of walls and yards, round grain stores and firepits, hoping to escape; but without mercy the ostrich drove her to the great kraal where Tsaxau lay bound ready for the knives. The ostrich stood over Tsaxau, and now the King, who had been called, came running and said quickly to his men, "Loose the ox there!" For he had not cared for the thing they wanted to do.

At that they cut the thongs from Tsaxau unwillingly, for they had made themselves want to cut his throat and his stomach and cut off his hands and feet and cut out his tongue. Tsaxau stood up and he put his arms round the she-ostrich and said in his own language, "Mother. My mother." But in some way Naledi understood, for it came to her that she had heard this word on the Hill Behind and knew its meaning. So now she watched deeply. The eyes of an ostrich are like a person's eyes and have long and beautiful eye-lashes. The ostrich gazed at Tsaxau and tears came into her eyes and dripped down her neck into the feathers of her wings.

Then Naledi said to her father urgently, "He will take the ostrich away, it is his mother, but let him not tell her that we have hurt him. Let the men run, get food, get drink, everything!" And so it was done by the King's word. Naledi's mother even gave Tsaxau a small iron cooking-pot and meal. He took it in his hands, wondering. But above all they brought water. And he drank and drank, and as the water went down into his stomach he seemed to grow and the tightness of his skin left him, and the great bird bent her neck tenderly over him.

Then Naledi took off the best of her necklaces and offered it to the ostrich, which lowered her head so that she could hang it over the feathered wing-shoulders of the great creature, whom now all could see. And the King gave Tsaxau a hunting-knife with a sharp iron blade. And so it was that Tsaxau left the Valley with the she-ostrich which was also his mother come back out of the magic pool, since life always returns, but not always in the same form.

All of the people had gathered and were watching, and among them was the betrothed of Naledi. She gave him a small look from under her brows. In that moment he was the swallow catching the darting fly, the leopard leaping on the buck. Out of him anger and fear flew, circled, fled away. There would be no curse on the wedding. All would be well, the honey loosed from the comb, the gourd drained to the last drop, the people at peace.

The Half-Person and the Scarlet Bird

It was a hard year, no rain until too late, the lands burnt brown, the bushes leafless, the cattle wandering, looking for water, their ribs showing, reaching up for branches or eating poisonous plants if there was nothing else. Even the goats were bags of bones, the she-goats could hardly feed their kids, still less give a cup to the milker. The poor farmer, Modise, and his wife were by now in despair. Their one cow was dead. They would have to borrow plough-oxen – if the rains came. If the ground softened. But too late, too late. The children woke hungry and stared at the pot and were still hungry after the spoonful of porridge which was all their mother had to give them. She was still nursing the youngest, the one in the carrying-bag, but the baby before who was beginning to walk, beginning to speak, he should have had milk. He should have had life. But he died. What to do, then?

Modise spoke in the night with his wife. They came to the decision that they must keep their eldest-born son to herd the goats and their eldest daughter to help her mother, but the next brother, Pheto, and the next sister, Lerato, would have to make their way to Gaborone and beg for their bread. That would be two less to feed.

27

So, very early in the morning, their father took them out along the path and told them to follow it till they came to the big road and follow that till they came to the big town. It was called Gaborone and many trucks went there. A truck would surely take them. And when they got to Gaborone somebody would be sure to be kind to them and give them food. So Modise gave them a little push on the way he wanted them to go and turned his back and went home to his wife with a sore heart. And the children went on, the boy with his little leather belt and a sling he had made, and the girl in her string kilt, carrying nothing, stumbling a little in the dust and stones and wishing there were berries. But there were none on the bushes; it had been too dry. Twice Pheto tried to shoot at birds with stones from his sling, but it was no use; they only hopped away.

Then suddenly there was a dreadful echoing roar and Pheto seized hold of his sister and they ran and ran until they saw a tree big enough to climb into it out of the lion's way. Up they went, sobbing for breath, and clung onto the branches. Pheto had lost his sling but what is a child's sling against a lion? In a while they heard the roaring again and clung to one another and held tight. But it went further off, and after a while was almost out of hearing. So they climbed down out of the tree. But where was the path, where? They cast about and couldn't find their own foot marks. Then they came on what seemed to be another path, and went along that. For perhaps in the end this too might lead to the big road and the town and food in hungry mouths. But nothing seemed right. After a while they came to a stretch of sandy ground, bare of grass, but with the hard castles of the termites here and there, and twisted dark mopipi trees but the berries on them dried into nothing. Here and there were biggish holes in the sand; had they been made by foxes or ant-bears? Some beast. Perhaps, thought Pheto, it was beginning to be time to lie down and die. Tears only made one more thirsty.

Then out of one of these holes came a movement and they froze, very still. Was it a hungry enemy with teeth and claws or could it possibly be a friend? Then they saw it had a somewhat human face, or at least half a face, for one eye saw them, half a nose twitched, half a mouth smiled, showing gappy teeth. But the other half was still and waxen and not real. "Come in," said the face and one arm reached out lengthily and the children clung to one another. Then that arm in its thin fingers held out a gourd of water, clear cool water, and this was too much to resist. Both of them moved and drank and heard the mouth mumbling, "Mmm, they drink, Mmm." And now they had no power except to follow the half-person down into the hole.

At the bottom there was a floor of smooth sand and a roof of roots and here were mats and bowls of porridge and honey and milk, so that it seemed altogether better than getting to Gaborone. When they were scraping their bowls, the half-person took another big spoonful out of the pot and gave it to them, saying "Mmm, they eat!" They felt full. They ate and slept and in the morning the half-person told them to shake the mats and scrub the bowls and get fuel for the fire, and this they did gladly. Lerato noticed a bird on the mopipi tree, a grey bird with a red head and breast and bright scarlet under its wings. It fluttered nearer and nearer, singing "Tshwidi, tshwidi!" But when the half-man came out of the hole it flew away quickly.

The half-person told them to bring in the bowls which had been whitening in the sun. Lerato asked if she should make porridge, but he smiled with the half of his mouth that moved and said, "No, no, there is good porridge made." Not only was there porridge, but meat as well, though it did not have a taste they knew. Neither of them had eaten so much before; they became almost sick with eating. Yet the half-person patted them and felt their arms and legs with his one hand, and said "Thin, thin! But soon they will be fat."

In a while they became very sleepy from all that food they

had eaten. Pheto said to his sister, "We have come to a good place." But she was not so sure. In her sleep the grey and red bird seemed to come again out of the mopipi tree and hover round her.

Because of this she was watching for the bird next morning, and sure enough it came, fluttering and inviting. She followed it a little way from the mouth of the hole, and there the bird sang:
"Tshwidi, tshwidi,
I was his wife
His wife, oh, till he ate me!
Look at the blood!
Tshwidi, tshwidi!"

And then it shook its wings until she saw the scarlet patches under them, like blood.

"Why did he eat you, bird? Who is he?" she whispered, but just then the half-man came out of the hole and away flew the bird. She did not tell Pheto yet, but it seemed to her that perhaps there was too much meaning in the way the single hand with the stretchy fingers felt her arms and the half-mouth begged her to eat, eat. There was sweet milk and sour milk with the porridge, but from what cows? Pheto asked if he should go and help herd the cows, but "No, no," said the half-mouth, "the cows are safe in the kraal. There is more milk, more milk, Mmm!"

The next day Lerato followed the bird quickly and it sang:
"Tshwidi, tshwidi,
I was his wife,
Look at the blood!
You too, he will eat you.
Will eat you up if you stay!
Take care, take care!
Tshwidi, tshwidi!"

But again the bird flew away when it saw the long single arm coming out of the hole. But Lerato whispered to Pheto what the bird had said and it became clear to them that they had fallen into the hands of a wicked spirit, an eater of people. And that night, while they lay on their mats pretending to sleep, the long arm fondled and pinched them and the half-mouth mumbled, "I am becoming impatient. Mmmm! They are thin but tender."

So the next day Lerato said to the half-person that she would take the bowls a little further to where there was a patch of very white sand to scrub them with, and Pheto said that there was a dead tree beyond this patch and if the half-person would let him take an axe, he would cut it up for firewood. So that was where they went, looking for the bird and now they saw it and it sang:

"Tshwidi, tshwidi,
Look at the blood!
Follow me, follow me!
Tshwidi, tshwidi!"

Then it began to fly, in short flights at first, looking back to see if the children were following, and then in longer flights. Soon they were out of the dry, sandy place with the gaping holes and the mopipi trees, and in among thorn bushes. But the bird knew the ways through and they ran and ran.

But then came a hooting and shouting after them and they knew it was the half person. They could hear the thud, thud of his one leg coming in great hops. They could hear the mumbling calling from his half-mouth, sweet names he called them, but they knew this was a sham, just as he was only a sham person. Faster and faster they ran, their hands and faces torn by the thorns, the bird fluttering and calling. Now, looking over their shoulders, they could see him gaining on them, nearer, nearer. But Lerato had been still clutching one of the wooden bowls with the white sand in it. "Throw it, throw it!" sang the bird. The long single arm, the dreadful fingers, were stretching, lengthening across the bushes, ready to grab. She threw the bowl and the white sand full at the single eye. There was a screeching and the fingers wriggled back. The two children panted on, so hot, so tired, the bird calling to them. Now they were in thicker trees, going downhill, and in a gap, suddenly Pheto saw the road, the real brown road and something moving on it, a truck – nothing magic, an ordinary truck. But how far, still!

For again the half-person was chasing them with the hop, thump, of his dreadful, powerful leg. The bird fluttered desperately, for the fingers had begun to stretch out:

"Tshwidi, tshwidi,

Cut, cut!"

That was the song Pheto heard and chopped with his axe at the fingers, chopped twice and off came three of the fingers. The dreadful thing was that the blood which came out of them was not red, but white and sticky like the sap of euphorbia. The hand withdrew.

"Run, run,

Follow, follow

Tshwidi, tshwidi!" cried the bird.

Behind them the howling was louder and nastier and yet the road, the big road, was nearer, surely, and nearer. When the hand stretched again it was seen that new fingers were budding. They almost touched Lerato. Pheto chopped again at the wrist but the light wood axe only wounded and there was a scream from behind. Between two branches the half-face showed itself, twisted with anger, patched with evil, the half-mouth dripping and snapping with greed. "Quick!" sang the bird, "The eye, the eye!" And Pheto threw the axe.

Now there was threshing and crashing and squealing in the bush, and again the children ran, but more easily, for now they were on a path and the road, half-seen, was below them. If once they could get to it! By now the half-person was partly blinded, first by the sand, secondly by the axe; he blundered against trees, caught himself in branches, with hoots and screams. If only his one great, hopping foot failed to find the path!

There was the road opening ahead of them, the road to

Gaborone where no half-person could exist. But the hopping
foot was close behind them, thud, thud. And suddenly the
bird ahead was gone. It did not matter, they were almost at
the road, they burst out, they flung themselves onto the
gravel. A boy was driving oxen, that boy couldn't be in the
same world as a half-person! And yet behind them were
faint and horrid sounds. "Which way to Gaborone?" Pheto
shouted. The boy laughed and pointed over his shoulder,
the other way from where he was going.

So what to do? They must try to stop a truck and get a lift
in. Yes, that was what their father Modise had told them to
do; they had seen trucks before; they were not afraid of
them. They stood there at the side of the road, but it was
no use. They signalled and shouted, but on went the trucks
and the poor children were left in a cloud of dust and stink.
"If only the dear bird would come back to us!" sobbed
Lerato.

And then, suddenly, on a branch above them, there was
the bird. But instead of being grey and red, it was red all over
except for the very tips of its wings. And how it sang!

"Tshwidi, tshwidi,
I was his wife,
His wife, oh, till he ate me.
But now I have eaten his eye,
Tshwidi, tshwidi,
Now I have destroyed him,
He will eat no more,
No more oh!
Look at the blood,
Tshwidi, tshwidi!"

"Oh bird," said Lerato, "dear bird, you have saved us!
Oh bird, bird, tshwidi, tshwidi, you are good, good! And
oh, you are all red with blood! But what shall we do now?"

"I will still help you, tshwidi, tshwidi," said the bird. And
now another truck was coming in the direction they wanted
to go. Suddenly the red bird dashed at the truck and flew

round the head of the truck driver, so that he had to stop. In a moment the children had clambered up behind and hidden themselves between two boxes. The truck started up again, they were on their way. And all at once there was the bird with them, sheltered by the boxes, preening its new scarlet feathers. For a moment it stood perched on Lerato's hand and she kissed it. On went the lorry on the dull, brown, safe road.

And then they were in Gaborone and the children climbed down while the driver was talking to his friends; they ran right away. But where were they to go? There were high houses and shining glass and many, many trucks and indeed other things with wheels and people, people, people! They stood against a wall wondering. All the other little girls wore dresses, and the other little boys had shirts and shorts; they felt naked. Soon perhaps someone would throw a stone. And then there came along a lady with a big basket. She was dressed like people in towns; she wore shoes. But she had a kind face. And suddenly the bird began to flutter and sing:

"Tshwidi, tshwidi,
What a nice lady,
What a kind lady!
Tshwidi, tshwidi!"

The lady stopped and looked at the bird and then at the children and a very wide smile came onto her face. "Is that your bird?" she asked. "Did you teach it to speak?"

Neither of the children knew what to say, but at last Lerato, hanging her head, whispered, "We did not teach the bird. It is Tshwidi, the bird that knows."

"Are you from the lands, little ones?" said the lady looking at them, and they nodded. "And you want food?" Again they nodded. By now Lerato was crying a little. The lady said, "I could take home a litle girl to clean my bowls and sweep in my house." So Lerato looked up and smiled. "And a little boy to dig the garden and run errands." Then Pheto looked up and nodded hard and the bird sang:

"Tshwidi, tshwidi,
What a kind lady!
Go with her, go with her,
Tshwidi, tshwidi!"
The lady went on, "And if the beautiful bird will some-times give me good advice, I will feed it on milk and crumbs of white bread and cake." So Lerato put her hand into the lady's hand and Pheto carried the basket and they all went home together.

Above the Whirlwind
for Amos Kgamanyane Pilane

When he was a little boy, Sengangarele really believed that there was a man with an axe inside the nasty brown whirlwinds of dust that sometimes swept through the village of Lekwatsi. His mother had told him so, but now he didn't want to believe anything that his elders told him. They were stupid. They just sat there. They had not been to school. They did not listen to the radio, but sang the same songs and said the same things over and over. They kept telling him to do things which he didn't want to do.

But when his mother screamed at him that the whirlwind was coming into the *lapa* where Keitumetsi was playing, he ran fast. For Keitumetsi was his little sister and she was the one person in the world he was really fond of. The wind that comes in front of the whirlwind buffeted at him, full of leaves and sticks and straw and pieces of paper, getting in his eyes; he was racing it. He shouted to Keitumetsi and she ran to him. But just as he was grabbing at her, there came the dust all round, choking him, and the whirlwind caught them both up, twisting him off his feet, while he held onto his sister blindly, pressing her face against his body. And the terrible spiral of choking dust and broken branches and thatch torn off houses pulled him up, up. And he was deadly afraid.

Then all of a sudden he was sitting on grass, rubbing the dust out of his eyes with one hand and holding onto Keitumetsi with the other. But where was he? It was somewhere he did not know, but it seemed a good place. There were green bushes and smooth rocks with flowers growing between. Keitumetsi wriggled away and began to pick the flowers which were showing among the grass, pink and yellow, violet and red and white. He took her hand and they walked on. Between the rocks was a little brown pool and here they washed the dust off themselves, and went on. And again there was grass, beautiful tall grass. But where was Lekwatsi? Where was dinner?

Then Sengangarele smelt cattle and over a ridge he came on a herd grazing gently among the long grass or lying in it, their jaws moving as though they were thinking deep thoughts. He came nearer, wondering whose they were and who might be herding them. The bull walked towards him and he seemed to Sengangarele to be the most beautiful bull he had ever seen. He was white with a black muzzle and black ears, a kingly dewlap and a great, even spread of horns. Sengangarele stared and the bull walked towards him, tossing his head a little and pawing with his hoofs. Sengangarele held onto Keitumetsi and picked up a stone; he was not going to be frightened by any bull! There was a heavy stick there too and he would use it!

And then a boy of about his own age ran quickly up to him jumping over bushes and rocks and signalling with his hands. But Sengangarele did not understand this. At last the boy was close and called to him urgently, "Kneel down! Kneel down! It is Kgosi. He is not pleased with you!" And the boy flung himself onto his knees. Then Sengangarele did the same, but still he did not understand. Now the bull came near and the boy spoke, calling the bull Lord and Master, saying that this new boy was a stranger and foolish, but he begged his lord not, on that account, to hurt him. The bull came close and puffed clouds of scented breath over them, and Keitumetsi put out her hand to catch them and laughed, and the bull gave her a long, warm lick, so that she laughed the more.

"Are you herding them?" Sengangarele whispered to the other boy. "Who do they belong to?"

"But are you blind?" the other boy answered. "They are themselves. How could they belong to – what?"

"I may be blind," said Sengangarele, "but you are stupid. All cows have an owner."

"*He* is the owner," said the other boy, whose name was Matsisi, and sloped his head towards the bull, who had now turned away from Keitumetsi and was moving towards a new patch of grass, followed by the cows and calves. "I serve him."

"This is nonsense," said Sengangarele, "but where is your village and can you find even a little milk for this small sister of mine?"

"I will take you to my village," said Matsisi, "but guard your tongue. If Tsholofelo has more milk than she needs for her calf and if she likes the look of your small sister, perhaps she will let her have a little milk. She likes my mother. My father was one of those chosen by Kgosi Mafetsakgang to build the safe place in the valley where we all shelter from the snakes."

"So you have snakes. Are you not more afraid of lions?"

"We do not have lions here, nor leopards, nor hyenas. They stayed at the bottom of the whirlwind. What came up were snakes with five heads."

"I do not believe you," said Sengangarele.

"Well, the time may come when you will have to believe." So they walked on through the green grass. Sengangarele carried Keitumetsi on his back. He wondered very much what had happened and where he was, but he was sure that the other boy was at least a little mad.

In time they came to a huge kraal, very well built, with strong, straight branches. Inside it, round the sides, were

small houses, granaries and fire pits. But in the middle was Kgosi Mafetsakgang, the Finisher of Disputes, with his wives and his young, splendidly horned warriors with their glossy, large-eyed cows. Sweet grass had been cut for them and here and there on tree trunk tables carved with the shapes of leaping heifers, were lumps of brown rock salt. They wandered, apparently communicating, touching one another. They were of all colours from white to black through red and tawny markings, and the fat calves danced around them. Many of the cows wore beautiful collars or head bands of bead work. They were all as clean as newly opened flowers and it seemed that the people of the village helped them over this.

Matsisi took the newcomers to his father's house, which was not large, but clean and sweet-smelling. His mother and sisters were making reed mats, pleasantly patterned. Soon there was porridge in the bowls, salt and cooked herbs to go with it. "Where is my father?" Matsisi asked, and his mother answered, "He has gone to consult with Kgosi Mafetsakgang about what was reported yesterday."

"And that was what?" Matsisi asked anxiously.

"It was a pair of the five-headed looking down from the great rock. Ten heads; they were counted."

"But Kgosi Mafetsakgang will protect us," said one of the sisters.

"Ah!" said the mother, "he has honoured us!" For there by the door was the great white bull and with him a man who seemed to be Matsisi's father, standing a little behind. The women all knelt, but the bull graciously tongued their mother and then the sisters held up the mats for him to see. "Ah, he is pleased to accept!" the mother said, and then the bull turned towards Sengangarele and Keitumetsi. It was not clear to them whether words were spoken, but young Matsisi nodded strongly and said, "Yes, yes, Morena, we will teach them the customs of the kingdom." Kgosi turned away and the next visitor was a beautiful reddish cow with a kind of brindle in her coat which softened the colour; she wore a necklace of blue beads with white flowers threaded through them. "Ah, Tsholofelo, hope of the herd!" said Matsisi's mother "Welcome!" And she laid her cheek on the cow's cheek.

In a minute she said, "Lady Tsholofelo has noticed the child and will give her milk, for the calf has drunk enough and must learn to grow up." She knelt beside the cow and milked her into a deep bowl, singing all the time. There was indeed milk for all out of the bounty of the lady cow, so that the porridge went down well and after that it was time to sleep. But Sengangarele woke up in the middle of the night and said to himself that it was all wrong. Cattle were only animals, yet people were honouring them and kneeling to them! He himself would never say Morena to a bull, no indeed! It was senseless. These people must be made to understand!

But it was not so easy. The next day Matsisi took him out with a basket to dig out and collect a kind of root that grew among the rocks. Some of the young bulls were there. Sengangarele picked up a stone and would have thrown it at one of them, but Matsisi saw and caught his wrist and twisted it. "Fool!" he said, "You could have hit him and then his horn would have punished you and reddened the ground before you had time to take another breath!"

"I wanted to scare him away," said Sengangarele, "I don't like being watched by an animal! He would have run – I have often done it!"

"He is guarding us," said Matsisi, "in case the five-heads come. Can you understand nothing?"

"I don't believe there are such things," said Sengangarele. "They are only stories told to frighten us!"

"Wait and you will see," said Matsisi, and then, "You are missing these roots. Look, that is the leaf. They are good with porridge."

"Do you never have meat with porridge?" Sengangarele

asked. The other boy shook his head, frowning. "Before the whirlwind came, I was eating ox tail with my porridge!"

"You must not say such things!" said Matsisi, "it is terrible, even to speak it in a joke."

"But it was true!"

"So much the worse," Matsisi said shortly and turned his back.

The roots were roasted in the hot ash and turned out crisp and sweet. Keitumetsi crunched them up. But Sengangarele somehow wanted meat and wanted to talk about meat, only he was afraid. That night there was a movement in the great enclosure and all the family crept to the door to watch ten of the young bulls go out, their eyes shining in the light of the fires, their heads held proudly. And then in the morning nine of them came back and their horns were bloodied and one carried on his back the front part of a five-headed snake severed by a sharp blow, but two of the others, alas, walking close together, brought home the body of the tenth, head hanging and eyes shut where the serpent had bitten him.

There was mourning and rejoicing, both. The wives of the dead warrior tore the beads from one another's necks and brows with the points of their sharp horns; even the dancing calves were stilled. But the remains of the five-head were thrown onto a fire and consumed utterly. Men of the village came out with bowls of water and washed the stains of serpents' blood and poison and the sweat of fighting off the flanks and heads and necks of the warriors. They cleaned the hoofs, each young bull laying one hoof at a time into the hands of his servant.

Sengangarele looked on and became more and more angry, although he had to agree that there did indeed seem to be five-headed snakes. "Some man must have trained these beasts to fight," he said, "perhaps long ago. And now they remember. But you have shamefully let yourselves become their servants. Servants of animals!" But Matsisi and his family were all so perturbed about this talk of his that none of them would speak to him. Keitumetsi, though, was happy and now, most of the time, she followed the beautiful cow Tsholofelo, all about, and picked flowers for her necklace and leant against her, both arms round the cow's foreleg, and Tsholofelo was always gentle and it began to seem that they were understanding one another, for Keitumetsi would come back saying that Tsholofelo had said this or that, or that the calf had played hide and seek with her. The family almost always had milk now, for Tsholofelo spared some for them out of her kindness.

More and more, Sengangarele wanted to hit one of the cows, as he had done often enough, at home at Lekwatsi, helping with the herding, carrying a big stick. He wanted to shout at them. One or two of the men or older boys would get on the back of one of the younger bulls, but only in play, only for a short time, since they would soon be thrown off, although someone who was hurt or sick might well ask for a ride and be given it. The cows usually allowed this privilege to women near to childbirth or with a small baby.

And Sengangarele was tired of roots and berries, beans or boiled herbs with his porridge. Meat, he thought, meat! He made a sling with plaited grasses, since there was no leather, but when he showed it to Matsisi and said he was going to kill a bird, Matsisi said, "No, no! The birds sing to us. You are not to hurt them." But all the same, when he was alone one day he killed a bird, made a fire, plucked and roasted it, burning up all the feathers. It did not taste very good, but he felt he was a man, he had eaten meat.

Twice more he did this, but the third time he saw a young heifer standing and looking at him, with an expression of puzzlement. Without a thought he threw a stone at her and she cantered off. But when he got back to the house he found grave faces. "What you did has become known," the father said. "You must come now to Kgosi to be judged."

They took him at once, and before the anger of the bull, Mafetsakgang, his knees gave and he knelt without being pushed. His eyes were on the ground and he scarcely heard what was happening. He began to wonder if horns and hoofs were going to end him as they had done the serpent. He began to be afraid down to his bones. Then the father of Matsisi pulled him to his feet and he saw that all the bulls and all the cows had their backs turned to him, the glossy tufts of their long tails hanging down, not moving. Only here and there a calf half looked round, then back. "You have been judged," the man said, "You have taken life. Also you have thrown a stone at a cherished young female. This cannot be forgiven. You must go back to the lower land from which you came on a bad day for us."

"But how?"

"By the way you came."

"And Keitumetsi?" asked Sengangarele, suddenly afraid again.

"She shall stay. She is the loved one of Tsholofelo. She will never become like you. It is only because you came to us while trying to protect her, that you are allowed to go back. We could have done other things to you. No, Sengangarele, you said till we were all tired that you are a man. Be a man at least now. Keep back those tears. And now, it is the end." And he stepped back among the cows.

At that the ground under Sengangarele's feet began to tremble and he felt a movement, a swirling and dizzying. Dust rose, choking, blinding dust and he was in it and being sucked down, down. He was bruised, battered, choked, could no longer think or see or feel. All went dark. And when he woke he was in his own parents' house and it was night, but a small lamp burnt and he could see his grandmother moving across it, and she was wearing the black shawl of mourning.

After a while he felt in himself that he was thirsty, very thirsty. "Water," he murmured. At once his grandmother came with a full gourd. He drank, but, when he moved his head, he was aware that he was bruised all over, head to toe, and he began to remember. But was it a dream? He slept again and when he woke dawn was beginning. Again he drank water. And then he looked round and whispered, "Keitumetsi?" But his grandmother dabbed her eyes with the edge of her black shawl and said, "My child, she was dead when we found her – when we found you both. Have you forgotten?"

"No," he said, "No! They did not hurt her."

"You are still confused," his grandmother said gently, "remember now, you ran to save your sister from the whirlwind. But it caught you both and lifted you up, and when it dropped you, she was dead and you were bruised and without speech. It is only now, after four days, that you speak to us again. But she – she is buried and mourned. The neighbours have come. It is over."

He could not bear it. He half sat up. "I left her safe – up there!" And he pointed to the dawn sky, growing lighter, through the door of the house.

"Yes, yes," said his grandmother, "she is up there, she is in heaven. Yes, truly."

"She is with Tsholofelo who is caring for her, who loves her! There in the green fields."

"Ah, my child," said the grandmother, "truly the angels are caring for her and there may be an angel Tsholofelo, yes, an angel named Hope. There should most certainly be such an angel. Did you dream this, child?"

"I saw it," he said, "she is not dead. She is only up there. They would not let me stay."

"We buried her," said the grandmother, "outside the house. See, there is the mound, there are the stones that cover her." Sengangarele looked through the door, and in the cold dawn light he did indeed see the small mound where the child was buried, close to its parents' love. He said nothing. What was there to say? But his grandmother went

46

on, "And you are still not yourself. We must make you strong again. Can you eat a little? I have a good stew here, made for the neighbours who came in to mourn with us, the best of beef. Will you not take a spoonful?"

But the boy shuddered and turned away, his face to the wall.

The Coming of the New God

The young man, Tebogo, came cautiously into the Chief's place through the narrow entrance in the low wall, beautifully finished, patterned with the careful fingerwork of women. It was most certainly theirs. Their houses faced warmly into it, the thatch well-trimmed, the water jars in the shade, the tall corn mortars in place, the wooden bowls and porridge spoons scrubbed and drying. Across one threshold were the poles; he looked aside – another son to the Chief.

The Mohumagadi, Morekwe, Mmaletlotse, moved out of the shadow of her house and stopped him, not with a finger laid on him but with a hard look. She was the wife of the first house, the lioness. "What is the news from the *pitso*?" she asked, as he knew she would. He was afraid of her. She had carried the Chief's seed.

"No news yet, Mmaletlotse," said the young man. "Only much speaking."

"By our lord?" she said, and motioned with her hand for the other wives to come out and join her, all but the young one, Boitumelo, behind the crossed poles. They had been watching. She was the lioness, their protector. It was she who had given them all the medicines which the *Dingaka* had made out of many rare and potent leaves and bulbs and which, taken by all together, rooted out jealousies and argument. They had been happy together. But now?

Tebogo began to speak, stammering a little, his eyes cast down amongst all these beautiful milk cows and heifers of the royal kraal. "He said – the Bull of our people said – that we were in great danger. These men with the guns were coming again to take our land for themselves and our young boys as their slaves."

"The *Maburro* – the Boers," she said, and spat out the Afrikaans word like a rotten fruit. She knew Afrikaans well enough but she did not care to sully her mouth with it.

He went on. "We have to have some kind of a something between us and them. Someone who will speak to them in the speech that they use. Or with writing. This man in the black clothes who came in the long wagon and who speaks with a loud voice – "

"The missionary," she said and again her voice was a hard spit.

The young man went on desperately. "He has said that he will be a shield for us if we obey him and his God in certain matters." His voice tailed off and he looked away.

"What matters?" she said sharply.

"You will know, Mohumagadi," he said, "as has happened to others of our peoples. Kgosi Sechele of the Bakwena – "

"I know," she said and half turned towards the other wives. "Kgosi Sechele was told by just such a missionary that he would get no help unless he drove out all of his wives but one. He did that. He was a coward. His headmen also were made to do this wicked thing. They were cowards. We are the Bamatsieng. We are not cowards. Besides, it did Kgosi Sechele little good. The Boers came. They burnt the houses. They took the cattle."

The young man said nothing. It was true. It was well known. One of the young wives began to cry. Her sister had been married to a cousin of Kgosi Sechele. He had been

rough. Sechele himself had sent his wives away honourably;
they were sad but their families had the cattle returned to
them. The wives could marry again. But this sister, not the
favourite but at least a true wife and no concubine, had
stumbled back unattended to her father's house, dumb with
not understanding. Some cattle had been returned later but
meanwhile her father and uncles had beaten her until she
almost died. She had not been able to explain that it was no
fault of hers. Her sister had seen her still limping from
the beating. Could that happen here? Among the women
there were low noises of pain. Then the Mohumagadi,
Mmaletlotse, looked round, motioning them for quiet. The
children clung to their mothers, silenced.

She asked, "Was he there – this man?"

"Standing beside Kgosi at the *pitso*. With his powerful
book. The book with anger. He said that no man must have
more than one wife. It is against the law of his God. And
if he is to be our shield the price is to worship his God. Also
we must use no more medicines for war or for rain. Instead
his God will help us. The ancestors, he said, are only dead
men. Also we must give him land for a house for himself and
also a great house for his God where we must all worship and
sing."

"I know this God," said the Mohumagadi. "This God of
the missionaries is a law to himself. He is an enemy to the
ancestors. He is also an enemy to women."

The young man gaped and was afraid. Women were
powerful in ways he could not understand but feared. When
they were hot they were as full of power as a gun pointed at
one's heart. He muttered, "He has this book. When he
opens it there is a pit of fire and snakes. But also good things
– milk and honey, he says, and cool springs. We shall fly
with wings. If we worship his God we shall never be
altogether dead. He will teach us to open this book of his."

"And what will he teach to the wives, the widows, the
deserted ones?"

There was no answer from Tebogo. A thought had come into his head. It might be that there could be more wives for the younger men. That the old bulls would no longer take the choicest of the young heifers. Perhaps that was meant by the opening of the book and if it was he would be glad. He would truly worship this God.

"Have I leave to go back to the *pitso*?" he asked.

"Go," she said, and the word was like a tree falling.

He slipped out through the narrow gap, the one that was easy to block. Had she seen him thinking?

The other wives came to her now, noisily, shouting or sobbing. "Sisters," she said, "sisters – we have to face this together."

"You are safe!" one of them screamed.

"It is I who will care for your children," she answered, "if this thing comes about." And gradually they became silent and the sun beat down and the tears dried and spurted again. They had been married to Kgosi for reasons of family or alliance with other tribes. There had been fears and teasings and sighing, but he had found ways to please all of them and had left none complaining that her house was not visited, the corn in her mortar not stamped. How could that end!

"We do not know what our lord will say," said one of the senior wives, a Mokwena.

"This that we have heard, it could be a story. To frighten us. In case we were disobedient," another said.

"Sisters," said the Mohumagadi, "we must wait."

But indeed and in truth it was many days of waiting and Kgosi himself anxious, not telling much, only seeking for forgetting-time and then the sweet sleep-time following it, to give him cover in the thorny and terrible thicket of argument and fear he was in. And word came that the Boers were gathering, they and their guns, far off still but their eyes were pointed his way. Yet each of his wives hoped that by this bodily gift of peace and sweetness to their lord they might avert doom from themselves and their children. But the man with the magic book and the new God stayed as an illness stays in the body.

Then one day without warning it came. Their fathers and uncles had been summoned. They were told. The young wife, Boitumelo, came out from behind the crossed poles, fat and beautiful and shining and her sucking babe the same, but Kgosi did not look; he could not bear to, being himself in the trap. There was a lowing of cattle, the rage of a driven bull, a bleating of goats, weeping of women. They took the babes that were still at the breast, slinging them on to their backs. But the older children were taken to the Mohumagadi and told, "There is your mother," and the children were very quiet and held on to one another. And in a little while and yet it seemed long to many as hurting things do, they had gathered everything into their baskets, all the things that give pride and strength to women, necklaces, finely worked skins, pots, cups, spoons, knives, all kinds of adornments in gold or copper, and sweet ointments, sacks of corn and meal, the hoes and flails, the tall corn mortars where they had worked together singing, the makings of their lives. And the Mohumagadi stood silent, not allowing herself one tear, saying go well, go safe, as they flung their arms round her before they went down through the town of Ditlabeng, breaking their fellowship. It was only the hate within her that dried her tears.

Kgosi came to her but he did not speak and she did not speak. There was emptiness round them. And then who should come but the man with the book of the fire pit and the flying people. He told Kgosi that God had approved what he had done and now that he had one wife he should honour her by taking her to his God and they would both together become God's children and God would protect and love them. He spoke at length and he seemed to know this God. The Mohumagadi stood with her head bent pretending that she did not understand, but in truth she understood everything and her anger fought silently with the cruelty of his God.

Kgosi said little, seemed not to hear. He was all the time anxious; he was hoping that the man would do good for his people, the Bamatsieng, in many ways. They were, he had heard, clever at healing, *Dingaka* beyond their own *Dingaka*. They could stop pains. It was said that they would make schools; his own tribe would learn to read the powerful book. And more especially there were guns. Better guns than the white *Maburro* had. Or so he had heard. But it was hard for him to speak of all this since the man spoke only of his God and also of the land which he would need for his Mission and for the church he would build where his God would look down and judge the Bamatsieng and their Chief.

Kgosi did not care for this; he was the only judge of the Bamatsieng, he and his elders and headmen in council together. If they misjudged, the ancestors might also show displeasure. But if the coming of this new God was the price – the missionary had promised to write strong letters. When the *Maburro* and above all this Kruger of theirs, demanded this or that in writing, it was always hard to know what was real and what was a threat which was not meant to happen. When one of those letters came, Kgosi became a little sick in the stomach. And his young men wanting to fight! They were his children; he could not see them shot down before even they had the chance to blood their spears. In a while the missionary was talking about this washing with some kind of water which would take away every sin. "You will bring Morekwe," he said, "and she should wear a white gown, oh so white, from neck to ankles. My wife will see to that. And afterwards she shall lead the women coming to our church in Christian clothing, to show that she has been washed and is clean in the sight of God."

But the Mohumagadi said nothing until he was gone. Then she turned to Kgosi and he could feel the anger at the back of her throat, since by now and in his deep affection for her, he knew her moods. She said, "My lord, I shall have many mouths to feed now. The children who are now mine. The girls will pound but I need grain. Above all there is need of meat."

He said, "How many cattle I gave back to the families with your beautiful sisters! So many. So many. Cows in calf. Heifers."

She answered, "Most certainly my lord would do all that was honourable." Then she added in an altogether different voice, "There is no need for my lord to buy me white cloth. If I must go with him into this water, if it is his bidding, that I will do. But I do not wish to wear this dress of the new God."

"It will be better," he said nervously, "and indeed, my wife must learn the ways of this God. Who, they say, is more powerful than the ancestors. Who has his hand on the rain. Or so it is said. Perhaps yes, perhaps no. It is also said that this God or his Son will take away any wrong things we may have done."

"I have kept myself clean for you, my lord," she said, "and it was the same for my sisters in their houses."

"Jesus – " he said, "Jesus – I cannot remember. The wife of this man will tell you what you must know. It is something that will help us all in Ditlabeng. Truly. And you must wear this dress. It is my command."

She bowed her head, the proud one, but her heart was not bowed. The wife of the missionary came, walking across Ditlabeng, nervously, glancing from side to side, aware that she was watched. Mmaletlotse received her; the woman was young and perhaps tender underneath her long dress. She had pale eyes. There was a man with her who tried to interpret, a Mongwato, but the Mohumagadi brushed him aside, saying she understood. "You understand!" said the wife happily, "You know Jesus! That is so good. Come with me!" So it seemed better to Mmaletlotse to go, lest by not going, she might be forced.

There were tents and two small houses, built hastily. "And there," said the wife of the missionary, pointing, "there will be the church, God's house, where you will lead the women to worship!" She spoke with great joy, expecting the Mohumagadi to show equal joy. But how could that be? And then, inside the house, she unfolded the white garment and held it out with smiles. For a moment Mmaletlotse was afraid; it could be a trap and besides she did not at all know how to put it on. And still she did not speak, not fouling her mouth with Afrikaans. The wife gestured to her to take off her necklaces and her skirt, which was made of beautiful skins, silk-supple and carefully sewn with patterns of other skins set in. The wife caressed the fur with her hand, saying how nice it was, not looking at the dark nakedness of the other woman. And suddenly a thought came to the Mohumagadi and she spoke stiffly, "I will give you such a one."

"Oh," said the wife, "I thank you!" She was surprised at the African woman speaking and also she was embarrassed, wondering if she would be expected to wear this savage thing. But it could well cover a chair. She helped the Mohumagadi to put her head through the opening and her arms into the sleeves of the white garment and she drew and tied the neck string. She had not been in the mission field as long as her husband and she shrank a little from African flesh. Yet she knew this was wrong and that soon this black Queen would be washed in the waters of baptism and the footsteps of light would move forward. All was as it should be.

It was a great day for the missionary, one about which to write back to his headquarters, when the Chief of the Bamatsieng, his wife and many of his elders and councillors came to be dipped into the baptismal waters. All the men had put away any wives they had beyond the scriptural allowance. Two of the Chief's young sons came, but another not. It has seemed wiser to Kgosi to leave one in the old

world, in case, after all, there might be a need for certain
ceremonies, above all the essential rain-making. Supposing
the new God failed. He did not put it this way to the
missionary and indeed shook his head over the unwillingness
of this son, Letlotse, who was, in fact the son of the first
house, the child of Morekwe, who was, because of him,
called Mmaletlotse. But that was not clear to the missionary,
although it was clear enough to the headmen and elders of
the Bamatsieng.

Yet some of them were sad that their Chief had been less
than whole-hearted over this matter. They were mostly
those who had suffered from fears and attacks of a certain
kind and now, it seemed to them, that Jesus and his yet more
powerful Father had made things so that they need fear no
longer. The night-movers, the *baloi*, had no strength left;
the terrors were over. Parents need no longer weep when
their children died; the little ones had been given wings. All
would meet in heaven, wearing new bodies without pain or
stiffness; eyes and teeth would come back. All this had been
promised after their baptism, after the touch of the waters of
life. They looked back with great joy on that day, and when
they began to feel fear or sadness coming at them again, they
could start at once to sing the new songs they had been
taught, calling on Jesus, who would most certainly hear.

But there was sadness in Ditlabeng among the cast-off
wives, sadness when women met at the wells and talked:
why had this happened? How was it now with the ancestors?
Surely they must make some sign! Some women who had
been sent sadly away from their husbands had been baptised,
but even so they could not go back. There were angry
brothers and uncles. Yet at least the boy Letlotse had stayed
away from this Jesus. And the Mohumagadi had been above
all glad about her son.

Kgosi came to her most evenings. But there were these
times when it would have been wrong for her to receive him;
she could have done him an injury through her blood. And if

she conceived again, she asked herself, what would happen
and how would the Leopard bear it if he had no comfort for
his loins? She was already past her best strength, although
she had never lacked for honour. But work was harder now,
all the singing and playing together had gone, and at night
there was no pleasant, laughing rivalry. Nor could she do
otherwise than wish sometimes that there was some other
sleeping mat where her Bull could slake his great thirst.

But a story came to her of how, after hunting, he had gone
back to the house of a cetain friend of his own *mophato*, and
had been offered the services of the wife – and that wife had
been one who, after her sad leaving of the royal kraal, had
been taken in marriage. How happy she had been to find her
true lord again, whom she had feared would never more lie
with her. Other such stories drifted through Ditlabeng; the
Mohumagadi was glad that her lord had found young
antelopes in what had seemed a desert; one of them, even,
was of her own *mophato*, true sister as well as fellow wife.

Meanwhile she cared for the children, saw that they were
clean and fed and that they swept out the houses of their
mothers. She told them stories and played games with them
in the evening when work was over and she could have wept
for the other wives, her sisters whom she had not been able
to save. Sometimes she would visit them, but one had gone
back to her own tribe and another was in a far-out village.
The young one, Boitumelo, whose *mophato* had been raised
ten years after her own, was still suckling her babe and had
not been sent into marriage.

These stories came back to the missionary. He rebuked
Kgosi after the hymn singing in front of his headmen; others
would follow the lead of their Chief, here as elsewhere. It
must not be. The missionary threatened to leave them all if
they did not serve his God faithfully. But that would never
do, since he had written strong letters to the *Maburro*
warning them not to come and to the heads of his own
church, demanding protection. Also he had started to teach

letters to some of the children. So Kgosi and such of the others as had sinned were shamed and made many promises.

For the Mohumagadi it was not to be borne that her lord was shamed by this man, so she remembered what had been in her mind ever since the wife of the missionary had admired her skirt of fine game skins. She went by night to visit a certain woman who was a *moloi*, taking with her two beautiful skirts, one of which was for the woman herself. Well she knew that this was now forbidden, most of all to those like herself who had been in the waters. But she had gone through them unwillingly, only because of her love and obedience given for ever to Kgosi, her lord, the Bull of the people, who was now, it seemed, to be tamed and ridden by this new God. No, she could not bear it.

She did not like to be with this woman, who treated her with all too much familiarity. She did not wish to be touched or to make certain gestures or say certain words which were demanded. When the woman put out a hand and pawed at her necklace, she took it off quickly and gave it. She had half thought this would happen and had worn the one she cared for least. Yet she was not pleased to know that now this woman owned something with her own sweat on it.

Yet in the end she had her weapon. She went to visit the wife of the minister, carefully wearing the Christian dress which she had been given for the special day of the new God, the long cloth skirt and apron and the cloth covering her breasts – yes, even her breasts where Kgosi had laid his tired head, where his babes had fed full and smiled up, milky-lipped. The new God, it seemed, hated the breasts of women. For a while she watched the men who were building the church and the new large house for the missionary. And for his wife? That was to be seen.

The Mohumagadi was welcomed at the mission. It was surely a sign that all was going well. A wife must be glad, naturally, if her husband is rebuked for sinning against the marriage bond. The missionary's wife was planting two little orange trees; she had grown them in pots. From this day they were to grow and flourish in the ground itself, the land which had now been blessed. She had been singing to herself, gently, as she pressed down the yellow earth round them, carefully making a small trench for the water they would need. Then came the Mohumagadi with her gift. They spread it out. She would perhaps not wear it as a skirt, said the Mohumagadi, but as a cloak in the cold weather which was coming. "I will put it on my bed!" said the young wife.

"The very thing," said the Mohumagadi. Yes, that way would be best.

So the days went by and the wife of the missionary became ill. There were medicines in the large box which they had brought with them, but these did not help. "What will happen, my lord, if the woman dies?" asked the Mohumagadi on a beautiful evening of warm dust and golden light, of distant singing, of her best brewing of beer. She went on, "Will the man go? Will he surely go? And will all be as before?" Kgosi said nothing at first; his fingers were on her breasts, warming her. She ached with the thought of the empty houses, the women waiting, their bull pawing and snuffing, at last entering and satisfying. How much she wished for a new young virgin, to be washed and teased and ornamented, to be looked over and touched, to be rubbed with sweet ointments here or here, to be offered and accepted. Surely, surely, this must happen again!

At last Kgosi spoke, "I do not think so. He will stay. Whatever comes to him. And perhaps he will become more angry about certain matters."

"This woman, his wife, does she make him happy. This one woman?"

"It is the command of Jesus and his Father. We are told that."

"We are not told about happiness. I wish this woman would die."

"They do not know why she is ill." He said nothing for a long time and the glow of light drifted up from the tree tops and the stars showed. There was a small chill in the air, the beginning of winter, the time of war. But the new God was against wars. There must be other things worked out for the young men. He lifted the gourd full of beer and drank a little, but not enough to stop his thinking. Then he said, very quietly, "You. Do you know why the woman is ill?"

She did not answer for a moment, but her breath caught and he listened for it. He held her wrist tightly. "There is something you have done," he said, and then, "I brought the man in, I allowed him, because we, the Bamatsieng, were in danger. It seems that the man has stopped the *Maburro* in their tracks. I also wish, for all the Bamatsieng, that there should be more knowledge. I wish that we ourselves should write these strong letters to the leaders of the *Maburro*. There is this also. The men who build the new church are getting knowledge. I do not care for the church but I care for the tools, the quick way to measure. We have bought guns, giving many good cattle for them, but we can never know if they are good guns. But the man will show us which will kill the lion that has broken into the kraal, which will bring down the fat eland. He will show us how, ourselves, we can make the powder and balls. We shall learn more about plants, about cattle and horses. Ways of digging deeper wells." He was talking almost to himself; she listened very quietly; it was men's talk. He went on, "Even if this man goes, another will come. We cannot escape, even if there was no good in it." Then he turned and spoke into her face, "Undo whatever you have done. I shall know."

And so? And so? Had it been useless? If all was as her lord had said, if it was for the good of the tribe, the thing was in her hands. She slept on her decision; in her dream something was following her. She woke early. She ground down certain leaves and roots and perhaps other things which she had, and made them into a paste with a little milk. She did not want to go to the *woman-moloi*, did not trust her to undo harm. Rather, she trusted in her own knowledge, gathered over the years.

On the ledge, at the top of the wall, where the thatch poles came down over it, leaving a space for air but not for thieves, there were bundles, carefully tied. She moved the corn mortar against the wall, climbed onto it, reached up and jumped down, sad that now she fell more heavily, just as now a night of dancing tired her feet. Yet there had been no dancing, not since the man had come. Had come with his wife. Yet should her anger have burned her fellow woman? The wife of the missionary would surely do only her husband's bidding. As she herself was doing now.

She shook out of the bundle the most beautiful of all the furs, not a skirt but a winter bed covering. She had treasured it. She put on the Christian clothes, slowly, shivering at the stiff, cold touch of the cloth. She went across Ditlabeng to the house of the missionary and, although she hated him, she knew she must not hate what was good for the Bamatsieng. The servant opened the door. In the room the young wife lay half awake, breathing shallow, sweat standing on her face. And, yes, the fur of the skirt which had been doctored was pulled half over her, where she lay, as these people did, between white cloths as though dead. Oh clearly, clearly, the medicines had worked. The medicines of the *moloi* which now the Mohumagadi, for the sake of the tribe, must take on herself. That was the dream's meaning.

Gently she pulled off the fur covering and gently she laid in its place the new and yet more beautiful one which, sometimes, had covered her and Kgosi in a sweet warmth. The woman who was in the room watched and saw that the Mohumagadi was feeding the wife of the missionary, and that both were smiling. She saw the Mohumagadi putting her arm behind the sick woman and helping her to sit up. Something good was happening. She saw also how the

Mohumagadi tied the skin skirt from the bed over her Christian clothes before she left the house.

In another ward of Ditlabeng the young Boitumelo, she who had lain behind the crossed poles the day the bad news came, bent over her baby and feared many things, most of all that her uncles would decide to marry her to a man of their choice. She knew who it was likely to be and she did not at all care for what might happen. At least it would not be until her little son was weaned. The babe of the true lord.

She looked up. There was the Mohumagadi. How glad she was! She brought meat and porridge and milk. They spoke together. After a while the Mohumagadi asked Boitumelo, "They have not yet made a new marriage for you? No? Child, you must keep that at a distance." She spoke again, "Do you remember the time of *bojale* – when we of the older *mophato* made you obey us?"

"Indeed yes!" Boitumelo went into giggles and covered her mouth. "Yes, with canes across my hind-parts! Oh how we laughed! I have never laughed so much! You beat me, my mother, my sister, oh you looked so fierce when I wriggled round to peep, but your cane came down lightly."

"It was only a branch," said Mmaletlotse, smiling, "but it meant obedience. Now I have this to say. It may be that I shall die. I would not have my lord, who is also your lord, going wifeless."

Boitumelo was troubled. "But Mmaletlotse, you are not ill! You must not die."

"It could happen," said the older woman, "and this is why I have come to you. My child, you are young still. It is hard to be the one wife. One must be strong, stronger than I shall be soon. And there are many children. They must be cared for, fed. They must not weep for their mothers who are gone. Do you understand?"

"I understand, Mmaletlotse. But I do not wish to understand too well!"

"I will go now," said the Mohumagadi, "leaving you with

this thing which has been spoken about between us. Which is for our lord. Which is for the Bamatsieng. Which if need be, you will speak of to your uncles." And for a moment she stood alone and listened inwardly, as though to something which might have changed its track, which might be following her. She saw also, inwardly, the face of that woman *moloi*, and fought it. But, having done one thing, others must come after. This has to happen. Lightly she touched the young woman on her shoulder, "Stay well, my child, my sister."

"Go well," said Boitumelo, "ah, go well! But if – if – I will do all that you want of me."

Out of Dark into Dark

Ofori had not counted on becoming Chief of the village. And more even than that big village, since there were farms all round, clumps of houses at the end of winding paths through thick forest, as well as a shrine which had a powerful fetish, and was also the Shrine of the Stool. It was well known over a surprising extent of the country, and had gathered round itself quite a population. His uncle, the Chief, had seemed strong and hearty, and there was his cousin, son of his uncle's sister, who was clearly the heir to the Stool and who took himself and his prospects very seriously. There was a younger brother too, standing between Ofori and the dignity he did not much covet. He himself had thought of going into politics; there was more to be made that way than by being a Chief and it was altogether more modern and full of opportunities. Meanwhile he had the garage and repair shop and did most of the hiring out of trucks and cars; he also owned part of the big store and would soon own it all, as he put more and more pressure onto the man who had started it, but had run into debt: his debt.

It is not possible to come to the top without treading on the faces of those below, though those born to greatness and

responsibility and acknowledged by lesser men, can sometimes manage it. If you do not care for treading on faces or if
you stop when they cry, you may end by becoming one of
them. But Ofori's great pleasure was to see other men
bowing and cringing to him and to know he had power over
them and to have people admiring him for what he did to
others, since that showed him to be a big man.

He had one sister who was not taken in by this. But she
had married a man of little account, a clerk in a Government
office who did not even know enough to help his brother-in-
law over a small matter of the alteration of a figure. Ofori in
turn did not help his sister and he beat his wife with a slipper
when he found her giving the other woman a small meal of
soup and yam.

For he had a fine house with pillars and glass in the door,
where his wife lived with their three children. Yet the house
he liked best was another house with another woman and
he bought things for that house which his wife had wanted
but had not got. One way and another, Ofori had been the
rounds of most of the attractive women in the neighbour-
hood, respectable young wives, school-girls, nurses, so long
as they caught his fancy; he liked to snare them with sweet
words and presents and then watch them find out that there
was no escape except through pleasing him.

All this cost money, so he was also in a back row of the
smuggling business, drink, perfume, many kinds of
profitable things and, lately, the drugs that go in small
packets and can be sold to young whites. The woman in the
other house knew about this, more than Ofori had meant
her to know, but there, she made him laugh. She made him
feel good. She was married to an old and stupid man about
whom she made many droll stories. He was wise enough to
keep much out of the way. If he had not done so, Ofori
might have arranged an accident, and then he would have
taken the women as his second wife, or rather his third, since
there was a younger one he kept in a small house in a far out

village, but she did not amuse him much any longer, so he did not often go there or see his child by her, about whom she used to whine.

No, it was only this one in town that made him feel so good. But he was not good, though many people did not understand this, because they were dazzled by money and felt that God must smile on him to make him so prosperous. So, when the road accident happened, and his uncle and both the cousins were killed in the smashed car, it was soon decided that the Stool should go to Ofori.

Ofori was worried. He knew in his heart that he was a bad man. His uncle had been a good man, not very good perhaps, but better than many. He had certainly tried to help his people and sometimes succeeded; there had been grumbles from time to time but most supported him. But now?

He became more and more frightened and this was something he was not used to. Old men came and told him what he must do. He had always called himself a Christian and had sent his children off to Sunday School; he had half laughed at some of the things that were whispered about the Shrine, though he had gone there once or twice for lucky charms. Now it was beyond that. First there must be the sacrifice of the white cock and then – No, all these things must be done before he had the right to the robes and the crown. No, he was now not allowed to go into the town or to speak with a woman. No, his car had been driven away. No, his business must wait. No. No.

He became soft, pliable, obedient; fear melted him. Had his uncle too been afraid or was it his own badness turning on him? He did all the things that were necessary. He swore certain oaths. He met the Fetish Priest and was sprinkled and clutched at and dizzied. In time he saw a little boy who wore a head-dress of gilded horns and above that a great crown of eagle feathers and gold on his neck and arms and ankles. The boy looked at him, but did not speak. He held a

69

brass box with brazen crocodiles on its shut lid. The Fetish
Priest said, "This is the keeper of your soul: the soul of the
Chief. It is safe with him. He is innocent."

The Fetish Priest nodded wisely and left them together.
"What is your name, little one?" asked Ofori, "and what is
in there?"

"I am Soul Keeper," said the boy, "your soul is in there."

Flames came out of Ofori, "In there – did you take it from
me?"

"It was taken," said Soul Keeper, "because, in a new
naming, the soul is in danger. It is no use being angry; let us
be friends." He said this with the greatest calm and softness,
so that Ofori began to tremble. He was a boy with smooth
skin and even teeth with clear milky whites to his eyes; his
breath was sweet. A boy like that could be a rouser of lust,
but fear was too great for that in Ofori. What was it, to be
without a soul? Had this also been done to his uncle? Yes,
for he remembered once at a durbar when the Chiefs came in
procession to pay their duties to the Paramount, that such a
boy had been so close to his uncle, sitting before him in the
cushioned litter. Soul Keeper. But it was only a name. Or
so it seemed then. But now? He clutched at his throat for a
long moment as though he could catch the soul with the
breath. Did the boy know something he did not know? He
thought quickly as though it had been a deal with a business
rival. Somehow he must get this boy onto his side. "This
soul of mine," he said, as if with sympathy, "Is it heavy to
carry?"

"No," said the boy, "it is light. It is too light. It is not a
strong soul. It must not for any asking, be let out. It must
stay here, at the Shrine. Only, on certain great days I am to
take it with me."

"Shall I not take it back, little one? Perhaps I could
strengthen it." He smiled hopefully.

But the boy did not return it. "Can you not understand,"
he said "you man who is now Chief, that many want to

catch your soul with sorceries? If you have injured people
they will try to injure you. It is for your protection now."

"But why now? Why am I in more danger than in – the
old days?"

Soul Keeper did not even answer, but looked as though
this question was too stupid for him. He put down the
crocodile guarded soul casket on the ground in front of the
shrine between his gold-circled ankles and began to play
softly on a reed pipe. It was the Fetish Priest who had come
back and spoke like a schoolmaster speaking to a stubborn
child, who answered, "All great rites put those who are part
of them into danger; you have been made bare before the
Stool. Your enemies will smell your bareness. Surely you
know that?" Yes, yes, Ofori did know and yet with half of
him he did not believe it, not with the half that was a modern
business man making money in modern ways and contri-
buting to the English church since that was the most suitable
for a man in his position.

So it came to the enstoolment and the day on which he was
named again and with the naming and the new cloth and
with the symbols which he must hold or look at, he found
himself becoming what was willed onto him. It was with
him as with a newly printed cloth in the market which
cannot be itself and bought and worn until it is named. It
was with him also as an image from the carver which is at
first wood and then a becoming, until it is named and all
know it for what it is. He was placed among symbols onto
his litter with the Stool carried before him; the poles were
lifted on six men's shoulders. On each side was a swordsman
and although he knew that one worked at a bakery and
another was a messenger at the Bank, yet now they were the
bearers of gold-hilted, powerful swords against the enemies
of the Stool. Above him was the umbrella of the Stool which
was covered with green and yellow and the flounce of it
orange. It was a little tattered, which did not matter, but the
bearer danced and twirled it and to Ofori's mind it was the

turning world of trees and sand with the orange sun circling
always round it. There was his linguist carrying the carved
and gilded staff, an old man whom he had laughed at in his
uncle's day, but now he knew the true meaning of what was
carved and he was content. There was a gilded hand carrying
an egg, showing that the authority of the Chief must be held
firmly but gently, not to be dropped, but also not to be
crushed. Before and behind were drums, enclosing him with
their voices. On the far end of the litter sat Soul Keeper, the
boy, with the brass box between his hands, and he smiled
sweetly so that Ofori knew that his soul was safe.

People came, people and people, to shake him by the hand
and speak good words and he wished them well. Most he
knew but some he did not know. Among those he knew
were one or two who tried to give him hidden messages and
these, he understood with part of himself, were about
money and opportunities, but on this day all slid by harm-
lessly. It was only when the enstoolment was over and the
palm wine distributed that he even began to think about
money, and that was strange for he had never been so long
without thinking of it. He was taken back to his house and
the Fetish Priest dusted him with a certain powder and went
off into the night, the Soul Keeper with him, as also the Stool
still carried on the head of its bearer. The sword bearers and
the linguist were no longer there and the drumming and
strike of the gonggongs scattered itself further and further
and the stars quivered high over the trees.

But his house smelt as it had always done and his wife
offered herself and now it was allowed and he took her,
though without much pleasure, and his dreams were mixed.
The next day there was much cooking. Guests came. There
was congratulation and good wishes but also business began
to be talked. Yet it was not entirely his own business. It was
the business of the village and the smaller villages. There was
a road to be built. There were the market dues to be seen to.
Did he know this and that which his uncle had promised or

had in mind? All this would need thinking over. But what came increasingly into his heart was less the good of the people whose Chief he now was, than the advantages to be had for certain of those from whom he had received benefits or might do so. But he found himself not able to make a proper balance, for things which had been said during his enstoolment came back into his mind and he asked himself whether his uncle, now that he was dead and able to see through stone walls and strong lies, might have to be reckoned with. Instead of thinking clearly about money, he was thinking in proverbs which were not always on the side of the money-maker, and this, he thought angrily, was what came of having one's soul taken away. Because, earlier on, when he was only himself, he would snigger at the old men speaking away in proverbs and hidden meanings which were often far out of tune with the things which mattered to a modern business man.

There came one of his old associates in the smuggling trade, with a proposition. "Not just now," he said, "not possible for me. The way I am."

The man was unbelieving. "A fine chance," he said, "your name not in it. Only your – " And he made the finger motion of money. "Big profit," he said wooingly and, when Ofori looked away, "The girl friend, she say she want – "

"No," said Ofori, but not so loud. He was wondering suddenly whether there was anything he had written, a small letter even, which might be used. If he had been careless at the girl friend's house. "Later," he said, "maybe."

"Later it shall be, Honoured Chief," said the man.

That night Ofori had terrible dreams, but in the end he could not remember them, only the wrinkled and greyish hands of the Fetish Priest and the white sheep's blood dripping like water off long leaves in the big rains, and sometimes the sweet face of the Soul Keeper upside down and the soul box with the live, jumping soul between his legs like part of him. He woke sweating and crying and his wife tried to comfort him but could not get him clear of his dreams. He wished he could send for the Fetish Priest to ask the meaning of these dreams, but he was not sure. Perhaps the Fetish Priest despised him once he was back in real life and no longer made different by the symbols. He knew that the soul box was kept at the Shrine, but he wished he knew where the Soul Keeper lived, for then it might be possible to come to some arrangement. Even to see his soul again! He began to look hard at little boys playing or running out of school, thinking he might be among them. Twice he followed a so-pretty boy, thinking he was Keeper, speaking to him, but he had not guessed right. One of the boys ran away and one asked him for money.

Yet this was seen and one of his friends whispered him to come somewhere and, when the door was shut, offered him tender boys. "Better than girls, yes?" The present to the boy should be this and to himself that, and they were guaranteed sweet and clean. Badness rose in Ofori and he thought what he would do to Keeper if Keeper had been among these half willing boys, their fingers cupped for the present. But that was impossible. The Fetish Priest had told him, and he knew deep down, that Soul Keeper was innocent, untouched and untouchable.

The proverbs kept slipping into his mind and sometimes the counter proverbs which are always there, until he became entirely confused. His soul was not there to keep the balance. He would agree to something and then forget, or remember it a little twisted. He could not, now, visit the girl friend, as he had done so easily, in that nice house, when he was a private man. Instead of giving him sweet words face to face she sent him hurting words by messengers. He was angry with his wife for being there where he was always seeing her, but he was even frightened to beat her now, so confused had he become. Should he marry yet another wife, a young virgin, would that ease him? But even the will for that was not in him, now that his soul was gone.

Sometimes Soul Keeper watched him; he would stand under a tree and the dappling of shadows would cover him. Sometimes he would be sitting on a step, reading stories, and nobody looked from the grimy school books to his face. Sometimes he sang with other boys in a Sunday School choir, for he liked singing and he liked to have to do with goodness of all kinds; he would sing, too, with the Moslem boys; nobody picked one open mouth from another. He would go back and tell the Fetish Priest how things were going, and he would weigh the box in his hands. "The soul is getting thinner," he said, "it does not move much. Should it be fed?"

"The cow's owner must feed the cow," said the Fetish Priest. "For easy questions there are only easy answers. You have mine."

"And the thing which is not the soul, does that also die, Honoured One?"

The Fetish Priest sat down beside his drum and scratched at it with his nail so that it hummed companionably. "Let us look elsewhere. A village can lose its soul. People go on living. Some understand the loss. Others – no. They only see they are confused and cannot remember where the good of the village lies. Perhaps a nation also can lose its soul. Yet men and women still eat and sleep and mate and go about their business."

"This I cannot understand at all," said Soul Keeper, and a puff of wind blew round him an airy drifting of silk-cotton floss, "who steals these souls? What has put them into danger? Is there some great sorcery at work? Can the souls not be guarded?"

"Some say this, some that," said the Fetish Priest, smiling at him, "but a Soul Keeper would need to have a great store of goodness and strength to keep the soul, even of a large village."

"Could you not do that, Honoured One?" asked Keeper, looking at him with big clear eyes.

The Fetish Priest shook his head. "It is possible I might have the strength, but certainly not the goodness, my child. I know myself, which is a cruel thing. But let us travel back out of the thick, knotted forest onto plain ground and consider what you keep in your soul box. It is, as you say, perhaps sick. It might recover. At *harmattan* time all green leaves are choked and brown with dust. Yet from the very middle of the banana one green frond lifts up in a green unfolding. That depends, not on you, but on the body whose soul it is. Should that body come to search for its soul, you must let him see it. But only here."

After a while Ofori ceased looking for the Soul Keeper. He began also to stop being frightened because of what he had become. Old badnesses came back on him and now he was beginning to use the new power he had as Chief. At certain times in the year he must do this or that. A message would come from the Shrine, which must be obeyed. Yet there might be made occasions for profit or influence. It came to him how Chieftancy could bring him what he wanted even more surely than if he had been a politician, since most people were afraid to speak against him in case his protections struck back at them. Some of the older men, who had known his uncle, tried to counsel him differently. They spoke of the needs of the village and the farms and how his uncle had busied himself about roads and small schools and a bridge over the river. "All will be done," said Ofori, but did nothing. He had forgotten the egg in the hand which must be neither dropped nor crushed. And people began to hate him openly and make up mocking songs about him, which he half heard.

Yet there came a day when he was summoned with other village Chiefs to meet the Paramount. The Fetish Priest had known even before he had been told and had come to make the preparations. He was almost abrupt with Ofori, gave orders over his head, demanded the best of the hire cars. Ofori sat beside the driver; his special cloth, his crown of cloth and fur and gold and his gold bracelets, along with other things which would be needed, were in a wooden chest on the back seat. As they left, he saw in the driving mirror that Soul Keeper was sitting in the corner beside the chest with the box on his knees; in the mirror their eyes met and Keeper's were sad.

There was a moment when he had been dressed and words said over him which recalled him to what he was meant to be. Soul Keeper too had been dressed to ride in the litter in front of him; he was a little taller, a little thinner; one could see what kind of man he might grow into; he did not smile.

"Soul Keeper, my sweet son," said Ofori, "is my soul safe?"

"It is safe," said the Keeper, "but I think you make it sick."

"If it is sick it is because it needs me, its body. Can you not show it to me?" But whatever it was that Soul Keeper answered, it was drowned in the loud and important voices of drums and gonggongs. Ofori planned in his mind to seize quickly on Soul Keeper, perhaps to make him drunk or threaten him, but in the car on the way back Soul Keeper was not there and it seemed to Ofori that the Fetish Priest was looking at him evilly.

Yet for a while he prospered. Then suddenly, like a storm out of the eye of the sun, the thing came. It started with one of his lorries in the road accident and the insurance had been dodged and the lawyer went right round to the other side and, when it began to look bad for him, everyone seemed to remember things he had done, they came storming and shouting round his house and some had torches and straw. The egg had been dropped and broken. Ofori made his wife go and speak to them and himself slipped out along the garden fence and through his banana plantation. He did not dare take his own or any car and his pockets were heavy with what he had snatched out of his desk. It was getting dark; he knocked against the rough thick stems of the bananas and caught himself in the stiff lower leaves. When he looked behind him there was a glare in the sky and it must be his house; he was deeply angry, but he thought more about the house and the fine things in it and the money still under the mattress where he had not had time to find it, than about his wife and children. And suddenly it came to him that one of the men with torches was the brother-in-law of his old girl friend. And there was another whom, he thought, he had got rid of. Hate. Hate. Now began his flight from hate through the other world where time had become different.

As he came clear of the bananas, up shot the Fetish Priest becoming taller and thinner, so thin that the skin and the flesh came off his face, and there was nothing left but bones and eyes. In his tallness he reached up and pulled down a star and threw it at Ofori, but Ofori somehow, in a heartbeat, dodged and the star buried itself in the ground making a scorching smell. Now the Fetish Priest was behind him and he did not know where he was running, only that is must be away from the place where he had been a Chief and prosperous and full of badness. His badnesses, remembered, made loops to catch him and he stumbled and fell, but got up with his hands out and full of dirt and gravel and somehow ran on. Many people seemed to mock at him, among them that girl friend who threw a bottle of perfume at him, but it broke on his head and the smell he was drenched with was like corpses. He did not know if it was night or day, only that he was running and so afraid.

He saw a church and thought he would go into it and explain that he had always put money into the collection and had sent his children to Sunday School – but were they alive or dead? But surely the church people would speak kindly and respectfully! Yet when he got there the church door was shut in his face. He waved money at it, but that was useless; nobody looked out, although he could hear voices and sweet music from inside.

After a long space of fear and clutchings, of darknesses and blinding sun, he saw his second wife in the small village, but the child in her arms was dead. As he looked at her, she began to change. She became a drum: inside the drum was the dead child. The drum began rolling towards him and he screamed and ran from it.

Now he was again in the forest. Across the path there was a trail of driver ants with their terrible jaws. They rustled the leaves, but it was not that, they were speaking to him, whispering, "Come, brother, come down to us!" No, no, he was a man still! He dodged into another narrow path between the grabbing green hands of the forest, expecting he did not know what. Someone from the smuggling business was running beside him, tapped his arm and said that Ofori owed him so many hundred cedis and Ofori desperately put his hand in his pocket and pulled out the money and threw it at the man. Then ahead of him he saw the Soul Keeper crossing into another path, carrying the soul box, and he thought that if only he could get back his poor soul, all this confusion would stop and he would be able to consider his situation and find a way out, as he had always done in the old days.

"All that has gone wrong is your fault!" he shouted at Soul Keeper, but he heard him the loud, bony laughter of the Fetish Priest. In his anger at that he leapt at Keeper's box and the lid sprang off and out went the soul and away through the forest like a small white squirrel jumping from branch to branch.

Now he was trying to catch it, imploring it to come back, almost touching it. His throat was dry from crying and screaming, his feet were cut, his good suit was all in rags and tatters, the papers from his desk were scattered over the months and the forest. He knew where his soul was going: to the Shrine of the Fetish Priest, and this was the last place he wanted to go, yet go he must. It seemed to him that Soul Keeper was beside him and now he was no longer a child. Time had gone by for him and now he was a young man who ran easily while Ofori laboured and fell and bruised himself. And here at last was the Shrine and before it the triple fork which he feared down to his knees. But the soul fluttered round it. "Oh soul, little dear one, my own soul, come back to me!" he cried at it. And the soul came close, close, and he grasped it. But it died in his hands.

"So," said the Fetish Priest and kicked him a little, so that he groaned, "that is that."

"What will happen now?" asked the young man who had been Soul Keeper.

"They will come soon," said the Fetish Priest, "and take his name from him. He will be de-Stooled. He will become nothing. Those he has injured will take their revenge and their money. Perhaps I shall give him a little work here, cleaning and plucking hens. Perhaps his family will forgive him, but they will not want to see him again. A fallen tree becomes full of grubs."

"They must choose another Chief," said Soul Keeper, "and name him. Is that not so, Honoured One? The Stool must be purified and passed on."

"Yes," said the Fetish Preist and now of a sudden he seemed to be full of benevolence, "the Stool must indeed be strictly purified." He said nothing for a time and his look went inward. He stooped to sniff at the ashes of a certain plant which were in a little gourd by his side. He muttered and Soul Keeper waited and Ofori groaned a little, but his face was in the dust. After a while the Fetish Priest looked up and it was clear that he was seeing what was to come. He looked straight at the young man, only casting a glance at the wretched wriggling Ofori, "That evil man was your mother's brother; between him and her was a great river running, across which badness does not go. You are the sister's son."

After a long time the young man spoke. "I have been

named Soul Keeper. I, when I was young. Can I also be named Chief?"

"You have had practice," said the Fetish Priest laughing a little. "When the Stool passes to you, perhaps you will also keep the soul of the village. For it is time."

The Finger

Kobedi had a mother but no father. When he was old
enough to understand such things someone said that his
father was the Good Man. By that they meant the Bad Man,
because, so often, words, once they are fully known, have
meanings other or opposite to their first appearance.
Kobedi, however, hoped that his father was the fat man at
the store. Sometimes his mother went there and brought
back many things, not only the needful meal and oil, but tea
and sugar and beautiful tins with pictures, and almost always
sweets for himself. Once, when he was quite a little boy, he
had asked his mother where she kept the money for this and
she answered, "Between my legs". So, when she had drunk
too much beer and was asleep on her back and snoring, he
lifted her dress to see if he could find this money and take a
little. But there was nothing there except a smell which he
did not like. He had two small sisters, both fat and flat-
nosed like the man at the store. But his own nose was thin,
and the Good Man also had a thin nose as though he could
cut with it.

Kobedi went to school and he thought now he understood what his mother had meant though he did not wish to
think of it. At least she paid the school fees, though she

grumbled about them. He was in Standard Three and there were pictures on the wall which he liked; now he wrote sentences in his jotter and they were ticked in red because they were correct. That was good. But in a while he became aware that things were happening round him which were not good. First, it was the way his mother looked at him, and sometimes felt his arms and legs, and some of her friends who came and whispered. Then came the time he woke in the blackest of the night, for there was a smell which made him feel sick and the Good Man was there, sitting on the stuffed and partly torn sofa under the framed picture of white Baby Jesus. He was wearing skins of animals over his trousers, and his toes, which had large nails, clutched and burrowed in the rag rug which Kobedi's mother had made. The Good Man saw that Kobedi was awake because his eyes were open and staring; he pointed one finger at him. That was the more frightening because his other hand was up under the skirt of a young girl who was sitting next to him, snuggling. The pointing finger twitched and beckoned and slowly Kobedi unrolled himself from his blanket and came over naked and shaking.

The Good Man now withdrew his other hand and his dampish fingers crawled over Kobedi. He took out two sinews from a bundle, rubbing them in the sweat of his own skin until they became thin and hard and twisted, and dipped them into a reddish medicine powder he had and spat on them and tied one to Kobedi's ankle and the other to his arm above the elbow. Then he pointed his finger again and Kobedi slunk back and pulled the blanket over his head.

The next day the tied-on sinews began to make his skin itch. He tried to pull them off but his mother slapped him, saying they were strong medicine and he must keep them on. He could not do any arithmetic that day. The numbers had lost their meaning and his teacher beat him.

The next time he became aware of that smell in the night he carefully did not move nor open his eyes, but pulled the blanket slowly from his ears, so that he could hear the whispering. Again it was the Good Man and his mother and perhaps another woman or even two women. They were speaking of a place and a time, and at that place and time a happening. The words were so dressed as to mean something else, as, when speaking of a knife they called it a little twig, when they spoke of the heart it was the cooking pot, when they spoke of the liver it was the red blanket and when they spoke of the fat, it was the beer froth. And it became clear to Kobedi that when they spoke of the meal sack it was of himself they were speaking. Death, death, the whispers said, and the itching under the sinews grew worse.

The next morning all was as always. The little sisters toddled and played and their mother pounded meal for porridge and called morning greetings to her neighbours across the walls of the *lapa*. Then she said to him, "After the school is finished you are to go to the store and get me one packet of tea. Perhaps he will give you sweets. Here is money for tea".

It was not much money, but it was a little and he knew he had to go and fast. He passed by the school and did not heed the school bell calling to him and he walked to the next village and then on to the big road. He waited among people for a truck, and fear began to catch upon him; by now he was hungry and he bought fatty cakes for five cents. Then he climbed in at the back of a truck with the rest of the people.

Off went the truck, north, south, he did not know. Only there was a piece of metal in the bottom of the truck, some kind of rasp, and he worked with this until he had got the sinew off his ankle and he dropped it over the side so that it would be run over by many other trucks. It was harder to get at the arm one and he only managed to scrape his own skin before the truck stopped in a big town.

Now it must be said that Kobedi was lucky; after a short time of hunger and fear he got a job sweeping out a small shop and going with heavy parcels. He was also allowed to

sleep on a pile of sacks under the counter, though he must be careful to let nobody know, especially not the police. But under the sacks was a loose board and below it he had a tin, and into this he put money out of his wages, a few cents at a time. He heard about a school that was held in the evenings after work; he did not speak to anyone about it, and indeed he had no friends in the big town because it seemed to him that friends meant losing one's little money at playing dice games or taking one's turn to buy a coke; and still his arm itched.

When he had enough money he went one evening to the school and said he had been in Standard Three and he wanted to go on with education and had the money to buy it. The white man who was the head teacher asked him where he came from. He said from Talane, which was by no means the name of his village, and also that his father was dead and there was no money to pay for school. The truth is too precious and dangerous to be thrown anywhere. So the man was sorry for him and said, well, he could sit with the others and see how he did.

At this time Kobedi worked all day and went to the classes in the evening and still he was careful not to become too friendly, in case the friend was an enemy. There was a knife in the shop, but it was blunt, and though he sawed at the sinew on his arm he could not get it off. Sometimes he dreamed about whispering in the night and woke frozen. Sometimes he thought his mother would come suddenly through the door of the shop and claim him. If she did, could the night school help him?

One of the Motswana teachers took notice of him and let him come to his room to do home-work, since this was not possible in the shop. There were some books in the teacher's room and a photograph of himself with others at the T.T.C.; after a while Kobedi began to like this teacher, Mr. Tshele, and half thought that one day he would tell him what his fears were. But not yet. There came an evening when he was writing out sentences in English, at one side of the table where the lamp stood. Mr. Tshele had a friend with him; they were drinking beer. He heard the cans being opened and smelled the fizzing beer. At a certain moment he began to listen because Mr. Tshele was teasing his friend, who was hoping for a post in the civil service and had been to a doctor to get a charm to help him. "You believe in that!" said Mr. Tshele. "You are not modern. You should go to a cattle post and not to the civil service!"

"Everyone does the same," said his friend, "perhaps it helps, perhaps not. I do not want to take risks. It is my life."

"Well, it is certainly your money. What did he charge you?" The friend giggled and did not answer; the beer cans chinked again. "I am asking you another thing," said Mr. Tshele. "This you have done at least brings no harm. But what about sorcery? Do you believe?"

The friend hesitated. "I have heard dreadful things," he said. "What they do. Perhaps they are mad. Perhaps it no longer happens. Not in Botswana. Only perhaps – well, perhaps in Lesotho. Who knows? In the mountains."

Mr. Tshele leaned back in his chair. Kobedi ducked his head over his paper and pencil and pretended to be busy writing. "There is a case coming up in the High Court," said Mr. Tshele. "My cousin who is a lawyer told me. A man is accused of medicine murder. The trial will be next week. They are looking for witnesses, but people are afraid to come forward."

"But they must have found – something?"

"Yes, a dead child. Cut in a certain way. Pieces taken out. Perhaps even while the child was alive and screaming for help."

"This is most dreadful," said the friend, "and most certainly the man I went to about my civil service interview would never do such a thing!"

"Maybe not," said Mr. Tshele, "not if he can get your money a safer way! Mind you, I myself went to a doctor who was a registered herbalist when I had those headaches, and he threw the *ditaola* and all that, but most certainly he did not murder."

"Did he cure your headaches?"

"Yes, yes, and it was cheaper than going to the chemist shop. He rubbed the back of my neck and also gave me a powder to drink. Two things. It was a treatment, a medical treatment, not just a charm. I suppose you also go for love charms?"

Again the friend giggled and Kobedi was afraid they would now only speak about girls. He wanted to know more, more, about the man who had cut out the heart – and the liver – and stripped off the fat for rubbing, as he remembered the whispering in the night. But they came back to it. "This man, the one you spoke of who is to be tried, he is from where?" the friend asked. And Mr. Tshele carelessly gave the name of the village. His village. The name, the shock, the knowledge, for it must indeed and in truth be the Good Man. Kobedi could not speak, could not move. He stared at the lamp and the light blurred and pulsed with the strong terrible feeling he had in him like a vomiting of the soul.

He did not speak that evening. Nor the next. He wondered if the Good Man was in a strong jail, but if so surely he could escape, taking some form, a vulture, a great crow? And his mother? And the other women, the whisperers? But the evening after that, in the middle of a dusty space near the school where nobody could be hiding to listen, he touched Mr. Tshele's coat and looked up at him, for he did not yet come to a man's shoulder height. Mr. Tshele bent down, thinking this was some school trouble. It was then that Kobedi whispered the name of his village and when Mr. Tshele did not immediately understand, "Where *that one* who is to be tried comes from. I know him."

"You? How?" said Mr. Tshele and then Kobedi began to tell him everything and the dust blew round them and he began to cry and Mr. Tshele wiped his dusty tears away and took him to a shop at the far side of the open space and gave him an ice lolly on a stick. He had seen boys sucking them, but for him it was the first time and great pleasure.

Then Mr. Tshele said, "Come with me," and took him by the hand and they went together to the house of his cousin the lawyer, which was set in a garden with fruit trees and tomato plants and flowers and a thing which whirled water. Inside it was as light as a shop and Kobedi's bare feet felt a soft and delicious carpet under them. "Here is your witness in the big case!" said Mr. Tshele, and then to Kobedi, "Tell him!" But Kobedi could not speak it again.

But they gave him a drink that stung a little on the tongue and was warm in the stomach, and in a while Kobedi was able to say again what he had said to his teacher and it came more easily. "Good" said the cousin who was a lawyer, "Now, little one, will you be able to say this in Court? If you can do it you will destroy a great evil. *Modimo* – the good God above all – will be glad of you." Kobedi nodded and then he whispered to Mr. Tshele, "It will come better if you take this off me," and he showed them the sinew with the medicine. The two men looked at one another and the lawyer fetched a strong pair of scissors and cut through the sinew; then he took it into the kitchen and before Kobedi's eyes, he put it with his own hand into the stove and poked the wood into a blaze so that it was consumed altogether. After that Kobedi told the lawyer the shop where he worked. "So now," said the lawyer, "no word to any other person. This is between us three. *Khudu Thamaga*."

That night Kobedi slept quickly without dreaming. Two days later a big car stopped at the shop where he was sweeping out the papers and dirt and spittle of the customers. The lawyer came to the door and called him, "You have not spoken? Good. But in Court you will speak." Then the lawyer gave some money to the man at the shop to make up for taking his servant, and when they were in the car he explained to Kobedi how it would be. The accused here, the witness there. "I will ask you questions," he said, "and you will answer and it will be only the truth. Look at the Judge in the high seat behind the table where the men write. Do not look at the accused man. Never look at him. Do you understand?" Kobedi nodded. The lawyer went on, "Speak in Setswana when I question you, even if you know some English words which my cousin says you have learnt. These things of which you will tell cannot be spoken in English. But show also that you know a little. You may say to the Judge, 'I greet you, Your Honour'. Repeat that. Yes, that is right. Your Honour is the English name for a Judge and this is a most important Judge."

So in a while the car stopped and Kobedi was put into a room and given milk and sandwiches with meat in them and he waited. The time came when he was called into the Court and a man helped him and told him not to be afraid. He kept his eyes down and saw nothing, but the man touched his shoulder and said, "There is His Honour the Judge". So Kobedi looked up bravely and greeted the Judge, who smiled at him and asked if he knew the meaning of the oath. At all times there was an interpreter in the Court and there seemed to be very many people, who sometimes made a rustling sound like the dry leaves of mealies, but Kobedi carefully looked only at the Judge. So he took his oath; there was a Bible, such as he had seen at his first school. And then the lawyer began to ask him questions and he answered them, so that the story grew like a tree in front of the Judge.

Now it came to the whisperers in the midnight room and what they had shown him of their purpose; the lawyer asked him who they were besides the accused. Kobedi answered that one was his mother. And as he did so there was a scream and it came from his mother herself. "Wicked one, liar, runaway, oh how I will beat you!" she yelled at him until a policewoman took her away. But he had turned towards her and suddenly he had become dreadfully unhappy. And in his unhappiness he looked too far and in a kind of wooden box half a grown person's height, he saw the Good Man.

Before he could take his eyes away the Good Man suddenly shot out his finger over the top of the box and it was as though a rod of fire passed between him and Kobedi. "It is all lies," shouted the Good Man. "Tell them you have lied, lied, lied!" And a dreadful need came onto Kobedi to say just this thing and he took a shuffling step towards the Good Man, for what had passed between them was *kgogela*, sorcery, and it had trapped him. But there was a great noise from all round and he heard the lawyer's voice and the Judge's voice and other voices and he felt a sharp pain in the side of his stomach.

Now after this Kobedi was not clear of what was happening, only he shut his eyes tight, and then it seemed to him that he still wore those sinews which the Good Man had fastened onto him. And the pain in his stomach seemed to grow. But the *kgogela* had been broken and he did not need to undo his words and he was able to open his eyes and look at the Judge and to answer three more questions from his friend the lawyer. Then he was guided back to the room where one waited and he did not speak of the pain, for he hoped it might go.

But it was still there. After a time his friend the lawyer came in and said he had done well. But somehow Kobedi no longer cared. When he was in the car beside the lawyer he had to ask for it to stop so that he could get out and vomit into a bush for he could not dirty such a shining car. On the way to the Court he had watched the little clocks and jumping numbers in the front of the car, but now they did not speak to him. He had become tired all over and yet if he shut his eyes he saw the finger pointing. "I will take you to Mr. Tshele," said the lawyer and stopped to buy milk and bread and sausage; but Kobedi was only a little pleased and he began less and less to be able not to speak of his pain.

After a time of voices and whirling and doctors, he began

to wake up and he was in a white bed and there was a hospital smell. A nurse came and he felt pain, but not of the same deep kind, nor so bad. Then a doctor came and said all was well and Mr. Tshele came and told Kobedi that now he was going to live with him and go properly to school in the day time and have new clothes and shoes. He and the lawyer would become, as it were, Kobedi's uncles. "But," said Kobedi, "tell me – the one – the one who did these things?"

"The Judge has spoken," said Mr. Tshele. "That man will die and all will be wiped out."

"And – the woman?" For he could not now say mother.

"She will be put away until the evil is out of her." Kobedi wondered a little about the small sisters, but they were no longer in his life so he could forget them and forget the house and forget his village for ever. He lay back in the white bed.

After a while a young nurse came in and gave him a pill to swallow. Kobedi began to question her about what had happened, for he knew by now that the doctors had cut the pain out of his stomach. The young nurse looked round and whispered, "They took out a thing like a small crocodile, but dead," she said.

"That was the sorcery," said Kobedi. Now he knew and was happy that it was entirely gone.

The young nurse said, "We are not allowed to believe in sorcery."

"I do not believe in it any longer," said Kobedi, "because it is finished. But that was what it was."

Out of School

They were at the same school, both wearing the school uniform, Kandisha, who was called Mary at school, in a blue cotton dress with the school badge on the pocket, and Chisalu, who was called Jason, in a blue shirt and shorts with the same badge. Both of them had two names, a home name and a school name, for two kinds of life which were sometimes very different and sometimes strangely twisted into one another. Mary at school was good at English and geography and history. Jason was not so good, but he liked arithmetic and above all he liked drawing pictures, especially coloured ones. Once one of his pictures was chosen in a competition and his teacher praised him very much. He used to look at Mary, busy with her writing, answering the questions, her tongue a little bit hanging out, her head on one side. He would like to have touched Mary very gently but he did not think he should. Sometimes they walked or even ran to school together, but mostly all the pupils went in crowds. He would have liked to walk hand in hand with Mary but he never did.

But then something happened. One day Mary was not at school. The teacher asked if anyone knew where she was or whether she was ill, but none of them knew anything. So after school was finished the teacher walked to Mary's grandmother's house, for that was where she lived. "No," said the grandmother, "I do not know where she has gone. She said that she was going to get her hair nicely combed and plaited by a lady who said she would do it. She thinks I do not see well enough to make the plaits nicely."

"But did she not come back?" the teacher asked and Jason, who had come with her, listened and was suddenly frightened. "Well," said the teacher, "I will come back tomorrow."

So tomorrow and the day after the teacher came again to the grandmother's house but Mary was not there, and now that she is not at school any longer we will go back to calling her Kandisha.

The grandmother sent messages and her sons came, Kandisha's father and uncles, and all talked and talked, and in the end it became clear to them that Kandisha had been carried off by a witch. So what was to be done? After much more talk and drinking of strong tea and beer they decided to consult a witch-finder and to pay him money to find the witch and make him or her give up their daughter. They talked where it could be heard, for it was possible that the witch might hear and become afraid and let their child go. So Jason, who was listening, heard this, but now that he too is out of school we will call him Chisalu. At school they do not believe in witches nor talk about them, but school is not the village. It seemed to Chisalu that whoever had plaited Kandisha's hair must have plaited in some medicine which would bind Kandisha and perhaps turn her into a ghost who would have to serve the witch and do everything she said.

Now the first witch-finder said only that he had seen Kandisha and she was alive and would come back. She had been taken far away, further than he was expected to go, and he might meet with a government officer. And he did not do the things which were expected of him, nor did he seem willing to go out at the right times. The second witch-finder said that if he found the witch he could foresee that there would be much trouble; he saw blood. The witch had strong powers with which to fight his own. But another woman had seen, or it was said that she had seen, the girl Kandisha going into the house beside the big tree which was the house of a certain widow who sometimes brewed beer and sold it. So, thought Chisalu this was the answer. This must be the witch. Why did the witch-finder not go straight to her house?

It was as though people wanted to accuse their neighbours and keep the accusations off themselves. They recollected words that had been said, or perhaps not even said – a certain look that had passed. That woman, for example, had a daughter who was not as clever as Kandisha. This other one had been refused a drink of milk by the grandmother and had gone away muttering. Only not me, they said, not me! That old man with the twisted leg – who, what, twisted it? And so it went.

But then it was said that she had been seen at yet another house. There were now two witch-finders at work. They had been paid three kwacha each. They would prepare the medicines, it would protect them, and go together at midnight. All must wait and watch; they too would be given medicine. There was a song, a kind of humming in the air. It went on and on. The witch-finders, masked and wearing medicines on several parts of their bodies, went out and the night grew blacker and the fear deeper. The medicines on the eyes and tongues of the father and uncles of Kandisha burnt a little. There was a thin screaming that came nearer and nearer. In ran Kandisha and at once out again, although her grandmother called out to her and tried to catch her hand.

In a short while, before it was yet even a little light, in came the witch-finders, stumbling exhausted, one with his mask torn. They flung themselves down and slept like the dead. When at mid-morning they woke it was a story of a battle between charms and the witch's charms won. It

97

was terrible, terrible, never before had they been beaten. Kandisha, they said, was not altogether dead, only a little. She was enough dead to be made to do the witch's bidding.

The witch-finders must be persuaded to try again. The father and uncles whispered together, counting the money they had. One said he would bring a goat. The grandmother wept and went out still weeping and told her two neighbours what had happened, and then it came to her dreadfully, could either of them be the witch? The neighbours with whom she had shared cooking pots and secrets and sons and friendship?

And in time it came back to school and the teacher told them that there was no such thing as witchcraft. There was only reading and writing, sums, songs in English, and of course football. Chisalu was a promising footballer, they all said so. But now it could not fill his mind. He went into the school and asked the teacher for a big piece of paper and some coloured pencils. Because she saw he was unhappy she gave them to him saying, "Make a good picture, Jason, make two teams playing football, and we will pin it on the wall." So he sat down and looked at the paper.

It seemed to the teacher that perhaps poor Mary had fallen down a well or been carried off by a leopard. Such things happened. If a child had to slip out at night. What was being said was not part of what must be believed in a new nation like Zambia. By humanists like herself. No, poor little Mary! Would they ever see her again?

But where was Mary? Or rather where was Kandisha? She did not know herself. Ever since – what had it been? What had been plaited into her hair that made her head buzz? She passed a hand over her head, where she should have felt the little black plaits sticking up bravely. She felt nothing. Nothing. She could not feel her arms, her legs, any part of herself. Was she then a ghost? She could not have been, for she was kept busy all the time, pressing, stirring, stirring. She could feel tiredness in her stirring arm, but she could not feel the outside of her arms. She knew tears coming up miserably from inside herself, dripping down, but she could not wipe them. She knew that she was caught, trapped, and there was no way out. How long must a ghost go on, how long?

On the paper there was no football. He turned it the other way. A tree grew, a great tree with large sheltering leaves and many-coloured flowers. Never before had Chisalu drawn so beautiful a tree. In the tree were birds; they sang at him. They sang Eat, Eat! The eater is safe. Safe. Safe. But what to eat? He felt tired, tired; he had slept little for he was listening for noises, footsteps, cries. His head bent, his eyes shut. When he opened them again the flowers had fallen in beautiful coloured heaps at the foot of the tree. But where they had been were fruits. He picked and ate and filled the pockets of his shorts. He had never before tasted these fruits. He walked out of school and straight to the house of the first woman who had been named. It was now mid-day, the sun hottest overhead. A time when good people were sleeping in the shade. No healer who was not a witch would gather herbs or heal people at this hour. It was not a good hour. But witches were busy. It was not for nothing that this woman was at the back of her house plucking a fowl; it was not quite dead but she held it down between her knees. She looked at him. He became as stiff as he could make himself. He said, "I am come in place of Kandisha."

"Ah," said the woman and let go of the fowl. It fluttered and staggered but it could not fly because she had pulled its wing feathers. Now it flapped bleeding stumps. Could she do that to – people?

"You are come?" she said. "You will come freely? You will help me. You are a good boy, a kind boy. You will help a poor old woman."

"First," he said "show me Kandisha."

"Come, come," she said and took him by the hand. Her hand felt cold and bony in his. They went through the bush to the place of burial. He had kept away from this always. In the heat of the sun it had a smell. And there were the piles of stones over the dead and sometimes things which had been left; perhaps crosses, perhaps not. If people all came singing nice hymns, many of them, early in the morning, it would not have smelled of death, even if they had brought a body with them. But now he and the witch were alone. But he had pulled out of his pocket another fruit and bit it and remembered the birds.

Alone. Not alone. There was Kandisha and she seemed very thin, very far off, and she was moving her arms round and round. The witch laughed and said to him, "She is brewing my beer for the other ghosts. You too shall do that for me. You too belong to me."

"Not yet," he said, "not yet. Loose her."

"Would you like to be with her?" said the witch, and made a smiling face, but it was not truly a smile.

He was becoming more and more afraid. If the ghosts began to shift the burial stones – "loose her," he said again, and he could hear his voice beginning to shake.

The witch went over to Kandisha and her hands hovered over the girl's head. She was unplaiting the little tight plaits one after the other. She was taking out what had been put in. She held these out on the palm of her hand and showed them to Chisalu. He became very unhappy. Perhaps the fruit was not real. He could not tell if he could taste it.

But Kandisha looked up and her arms stopped turning. She did not know where she was. She looked round and first she was looking at a burial mound and then she was looking at Chisalu. "Run!" he said. "Run!" And then, "Mary, it is late. Run to school!" And suddenly she burst out of the burial ground, back, back, rushing through the bushes, not caring for falls.

"And now," said the witch. "Come, come!" And she beckoned to him.

But then a bird stirred in one of the bushes which Kandisha had shaken and it sang "Eat! Eat!" And he pulled the last of the fruits out of his pocket and crushed it between his teeth and felt the taste.

And at the same time he heard singing of a certain kind and he knew it must be the witch-finders coming, since they too worked at mid-day and midnight, finding what they were looking for. And the witch also heard what he had heard and suddenly she became not now frightening, but changed to someone herself very frightened, very easy to hurt, and suddenly she ran the other way into the thick bush. And when the witch-finders came, what they found was Chisalu and he was shaking and pointing.

One of Kandisha's uncles had followed; he was a big man. He picked up Chisalu, although he was a half grown boy. He smelled not of burial ground but of wood shavings, because he was a carpenter. Wood shavings and iron tools and real beer, not the scentless sweet beer of ghosts.

When they got back to the village who was there but the teacher, holding Kandisha by the hand. "Poor Mary," she said to the grandmother, "she has been lost in the bush. She can't remember anything. She must not be bothered or questioned. I gave her milk and porridge at school. Poor Mary, her hair is all loose, full of thorns and leaves!" And she whispered to the grandmother, "Let her sleep as long as you can. She is not bewitched, only she has been dreadfully frightened. And tomorrow she should come back to school and I will look after her."

So the grandmother spread a mat in the inner room and sat down beside Kandisha till she went to sleep. And there she slept and slept and came entirely back from being a ghost. But the witch had rushed deep into the bush and when she came back to the village she had no house, no nothing, only ashes, and her neighbours shouting at her and throwing stones. Most of all the others who had been accused themselves of witchcraft.Everyone praised the witch-finders and Chisalu kept very quiet. He knew best, but it is often not wise to speak.

The next day the teacher said, "What a fine picture you did of the football teams, Jason! I shall put it on the wall."

"Did I make football?" he said, puzzled.

"Of course," she said, and showed him the picture he had made. There was no tree, no birds, no fruit. Instead there were two teams and a ball high in the air and boys jumping and reaching up for it.

"But what," she said, "are those two piles of coloured things? You have made nice colours but it is not clear."

Yes, he thought, those are the flowers falling off the tree, but there is no tree. They must be something else. So he looked hard and said, "But these are the footballers' jerseys. It is a hot day. They have taken them off. They put them into two heaps, one for each team."

"Of course," said the teacher. "Yes, of course that is what you have made and it looks so nice, Jason. Perhaps I shall send it in for a competition. Of course, football jerseys!"

Football jerseys. Yes, football jerseys, of course. What else?

Father and Son

His father was a Zionist: therefore his mother died. He had been a young boy at the time and the look on his mother's face when they opened the door of the hut, where she had been put with the door barred to all but the healers, shook him to the heart. Later he pieced together what had happened. It seemed she had a miscarriage and much bleeding so they had taken her away and prayed over her and given her nothing but heavily salted water to drink in order to take the evil out of her. So that she died, as it were, of thirst. After that he hated home. He had wanted to stay on at school but his father only wanted him to stay there until he could read the word aloud. For his father was going blind; later, when he was a man, Maikutlo thought that his father could have saved his sight if he had been willing to go to a hospital and have the operation. But naturally a Zionist could not do that.

Maikutlo managed an extra grade at school by pretending that he could not yet read well enough and when he had at last to read aloud every day he cleverly altered the words even from his father's Bible so that all became a little frightening and yet his father was not able to understand what he was doing. When his father was truly frightened, sweating with fear, Maikutlo thought of his mother and the fear in which she must have died. Was it heaven she went to? He did not think so unless heaven was only the escape from hell on earth. Sometimes he tried to go without drinking water or milk so as to know how his mother had died, that surely was hell.

Then suddenly he was tired of this fear game. He ran away from home, taking all the money he could find. He wished there had been a picture of his mother but there was only the wedding photograph and his father was in that so he did not like it. Besides, she looked sad and he wanted to remember her laughing, as she had been when he was a little boy and she ran after him and caught him and hugged him. Sometimes he thought his young sister Lempaletse looked a little like her, the small sister whom he must leave to tend the house and the half blind father who at least seldom hit her with his stick though he tried to often enough.

After a while Maikutlo was working in a garage. He had thrown away the black Zionist star which had been pinned on his shirt ever since he had a shirt to wear. It seemed that he could read instructions and be trusted to carry them out; he could remember the names of spare parts and tools. Where he was there were no other Zionists and if he saw the Zionist badge on anyone he would if possible treat that person badly. But he thought he must have been baptised into the Zionist church and that thought hurt him. Sometimes he dreamed about his father and in the dream killed him.

Slowly it became known that Maikutlo was the best mechanic at the garage. People asked for him specially and gave him money for himself. So in a while he had first money in a tin and then a savings account and a girl friend who worked in a shop selling such delicate things as scarves and stockings and small bracelets. She was a kind and merry girl and after a while she fell pregnant. She meant to go back to her village where her mother, after scolding and perhaps beating her, would take the baby. But Maikutlo said they should get married. He went to her uncle and showed the savings book but said that he was an orphan without family. The uncle accepted him and gave a wedding party and as soon as he was married he began to love his wife more and more. When her belly had become altogether too big they could still caress one another and melt into tenderness. So the time came for her to give birth and she had a baby boy and all was joy in their small house. Yet this did not last for long. Maikutlo's wife became suddenly ill. He got her to the hospital, but all the same she died. Her mother took the child and Maikutlo went back into hatred and unhappiness, the worst time of his life, from which his only way out was by the skill of brains and hand with his work on engines. It was because of this that the engineer who was in charge of building the new chain of dams took him on as his own driver.

Now after a while they began to speak and it was not altogether as master and man, but rather as two men, and now Maikutlo was addressing the engineer before others as "sir" but when they were alone as Johnny. They spoke in the evenings when they were camping at the dam site, sometimes of the stars and of the animals whom they could hear or smell, and much also of the machines, especially the great elephant machines that scooped the soil and even big rocks and took all over to the dam walls. Once Johnny had taken him to such a machine and showed him the controls and it became clear to Maikutlo that some day he would be driving one but yet he also liked to be driving and looking after the boss truck with Johnny. He did not respect him less at these times of talk when also he was able to question him, mostly about his work. He had been vastly surprised at the way that Johnny always went to the Chief wherever he was working and asked that a meeting should be held. He would then make a great explanation and ask for questions and ideas, especially about the siting of the dam, and after the meeting he would wait for a day, since perhaps those who knew best about weather and soil and the history of the place were shy to come forward at first. And he always listened to them. So one day, sitting beside a track through the bush and drinking tea together, Maikutlo asked, "Why is it that you, Johnny, who have so much knowledge and power should listen to these ignorant people?"

So Johnny said, "One should always listen to others. They may have something very good to tell, very important. Not once only but several times I have altered my plans because someone gave me a reason."

"But you need not have done that."

Johnny stayed quiet for a time, then he turned halfway from Maikutlo. He said, "Once when I was a young man, but it was in another part of Africa, I built a dam and I did not listen to those who understood the way rain might come. If I had listened the spillway would have been built differently. Then the dam wall burst. It was not a large dam but there was a child drowned. I have never forgotten."

"Oh," said Maikutlo, "my father! Even you have known sorrow."

Johnny nodded, stood up, got back into the truck, but it seemed to Maikutlo that there had been a sudden closeness although no more would be said. So the days went on and sometimes Maikutlo dreamed of his dead wife and sometimes he wished sadly, sadly to see his child. But how could he look after a baby boy? He must leave him with the old woman, even though visiting her made his heart sore because she reminded him of what he had lost. Once or twice he spoke to the engineer about his little son but he did not speak of his wife; that would have hurt too much. And yet he half thought that Johnny understood.

Then one day at the end of the driving they had come near to the village which Maikutlo had left in the second worst time of his life. And then he thought suddenly of his little sister Lempaletse. What had become of her? Was she still looking after the old man or had she married, she must be coming up to that age?

He asked for leave to see his relatives and went to the village. He knew the way only too well, although trees had grown and here and there houses had been built or pulled down. His feet went slowly. He came to his father's house and there yes, there was his sister pounding away for porridge, taller than she had been, barefoot, badly dressed. From the wall of the *lapa* he greeted her and she cried out and dropped the heavy wooden pestle out of the corn mortar. Quickly she got his news and he hers. Both were unhappy. It seemed that the father intended to marry Lempaletse to an old friend of his, a man his own age, a widower greedy for a young wife. She had been trying by all means to put this off.

All became suddenly clear to Maikutlo. "Come away with me and take care of my child. When he can run I will let you marry the man you will choose for yourself."

"Yes," she said, "yes, my brother – if our father lets me go!"

He took her by the hand and together they went to speak to their father who was by now totally blind and had a bad smell. It was not a good talk. Maikutlo had to say how his beautiful wife had died. The old man said, "That was your fault! You did wrong. You should have prayed. You should have called in the elders and healers of the church."

"I am no longer in that church," said Maikutlo, and he was beginning to feel such hatred and disgust at his father that he could barely stand still.

"Judas, you!" said his father, "you killed your wife!" But Maikutlo could not bear it, not that. He hit his blind father full in the face so that he almost fell. He caught his sister by the wrist and dragged her after him. He ran down the road, away, away, pulling her tightly, though she ran with him sobbing but not crying out for she wanted to go.

At a turn of the road, once clear out of sight, he stopped,

panting. "I hit him," he said, "I hit my old blind father. Did you see?"

"I saw," she said, "it is true. That is what you did. It is a terrible thing for any man to have done. God will see. He will punish us both. You and me; I did not stay to help him. And now?"

"God has not seen," he said. "That God is dead." And then: "Take that off!" And he tugged at the black Zionist star over her small breast. "Now, throw it away! Far, far! You cannot go back now."

They went quickly, half running, but Lempaletse was afraid, for she could not believe him. But had he spoken truth? Had he not done a great wickedness, striking his own father on the flesh? No, he said to himself, this was justice which is stronger than the tying together by blood. But did he altogether believe that? No.

So they came back to the engineer's camp. Now Lempaletse held back and cried a little. "That is the truck", he said. "You will sleep in the back of it. I will bring blankets."

"But I am afraid! Will God see me now that – that – I have lost my star?"

"It is I who will care for you, my sister, and you must stop thinking of that God, and of that star!"

"But I hope God did not see you strike our father!"

"I had the right to strike him," said Maikutlo, and helped his sister into the truck and tucked the blanket round her. But in his heart he was still not happy since he had done something which no Motswana should do, however provoked. He, the only son, had done this.

So the next morning he showed Lempaletse to the engineer, saying that this was indeed his sister who would look after the baby, his son, until he was old enough to come with his father.

"That's okay," said Johnny, and greeted Lempaletse, to which she was too shy to do more that whisper back. "See that she eats well while she is with us." And then he said: "You'll be feeling better now, Maikutlo."

For a moment Maikutlo did not answer but scuffed with his foot in the sand. Then he said, "I struck him: my father, an old man, blind."

Instead of rebuking him Johnny said: "Why did you do that?"

"I hated him."

"Because of what?"

Slowly he spoke: about his childhood, about what had happened. Fully. The foreman came up, but Johnny the engineer motioned with his hand, checking him. And as it all came draining out of Maikutlo the hatred seemed to drain as well, until he was like the bed of a lake whose dam had burst leaving a strange smooth ground with only the dead remains of anger like the spiked branches of old water-blackened trees that lie on the green-mottled mud until the roaming cattle break them into small splinters. And as his hate left him so did the guilt of the blow. All had gone away as the water from the broken dam goes, sinking without trace into the ground. "It is not good to hate", said the engineer. "It comes between oneself and what one is doing. Maikutlo, I did not know for sure about your wife although I had guessed a little. Even less did I know about your mother. Now I know all." He laid his hand for a moment lightly and cheeringly on Maikutlo's hand. "Grief also should not go on forever. And soon your son will need you."

"I understand," Maikutlo whispered back and then: "I thank you, my father, Johnny my father, my new father who has become." And then he stepped aside for the foreman who was becoming impatient.

The Order of Earth

The old man said, "I come from the shrine."

The young woman in the pink frills over brown bosom, and who was she anyhow, said, "What shrine?" And she yawned in his face. Her breath smelt of spirits. Her bosom smelt of something not woman, not human, some foreign thing. He loathed it.

"He will know. Tell your master."

"No master of mine," said the young woman. "Me, I don't have masters."

He spoke out of the night he had come in: "You too will be sorry if he gets no message."

The young woman hesitated, looked back over her shoulder, took a chew into her mouth, was afraid. The old man had a small white beard like some kind of monkey, his white robe ordinary, but the staff in his hand – one could not afford to ignore some things. She called back into the house, pulling the curtain a little – ah, that curtain, what money it cost, the real gold thread! – and spoke in English, calling him by his Mission name, Paul. Safer that way.

"Tell him, go away," was the answer, but she did not pass it on. Instead she was more urgent: "You come, self." So at last it was the master of the house, in his real-silk pyjama trousers and his massive bare top, shining, heavy, for the moment hers, in exchange for the bosom and all else. He would never be content with less than all, in a deal or a girl. But that was all right by her, up to now. He shouldered past her, breathing bull-like, stood four-square. "Go away, you," he said.

The old man lifted his stick, just a little, "I am from the place you know. I come to give you one more chance."

"Give me! Listen, I am big. I take chances. Take them!"

"That does not do with the Gods. Man cannot only take. It is known that you have taken too much. Giving none back to Earth."

"Your old Gods – village nonsense!"

But the young woman put her hand over his mouth and whispered urgently, "Give him money! He will curse you unless – I am not waiting here to be cursed! Getting your purse." She hurried back into the room, felt under the pillow, he liked to keep it there, yes, like a village man, would pull it out when she was flat and panting, put a big paper money between legs or lips. She fled back with it. But the old man was holding his hand up to his head. "Oh Paul, what you do!"

"Didn't mean to hit him," Paul said, "but he got me annoyed. Knows plenty too much about my deals. Says I break something. *Ogiyan* says."

"Did he speak about me?" the young woman asked anxiously. "Did he say you break Commandment?"

"No! He is not interested. Does not care about women. Not Mission, him. You don't count."

She was relieved – and hurt. "But I do count, Paul, with you? Here, give him money, plenty, that will heal his head." She shoved the purse into his hand. "Give him big money – you have it to give!" She stepped back, wanting to be out of range. Some people said she was sinning, so she gave money to her own church which had its own powerful Jesus Book of cursing and washings, and always, after the money and the praying she got washed, so she could go on sinning from fresh. But maybe this was different. From something older, stronger, outside the city. She did not like to hear about the Gods, she did not want to remember their stories which could be daylight true. Not just dreams. Dreams of fright and hunt, and a bad smell, and something she didn't know had to be done.

It had been just first light when the old man had come and knocked so hard she had to answer. It was full light now. Day. Nothing bad happens in full day, everyone knows that. Not in a big city. Million people, more. Million cars, almost. Not like a village place where the earth things show through. Because it was so big a city Paul could do his things, new kind of things, to do with oil, what did she know? Foreigners came and helped him, he did not even pay them, he was developing country, not so? She thought hard. If this old man was taking money from some not-friend of Paul, someone who had lost out on a deal, well, could it be that? Maybe the foreign adviser would help, or would he not believe? Or was it worse – had Paul talked and laughed too loud? So that they, whoever they were, heard, back, wherever it was. So that they would look in his heart.

She got into bed, safe there. In a while he came. He had the purse. "He took the money, Paul? Took it right?" But the big man shook his head. She poured a drink, a stiff one. "Come now, fuck me good. Make my titties stand. Forget all this!" But it was not a good one. Neither his mind nor any part of his body was truly forgetting. Over quick. Hardly a sin, even.

He was not himself all that day, and the hours of it seemed to stretch, long, long. She begged him, send for the foreign adviser, but he said no, it was not to be spoken about. "Nobody is to come in," he said, "Put up all the bars." And then, to her, "You. Do not open. Whatever is said to you. Or given."

"You stop trusting me, then?" she said. "Paul, you think

I'd take a present? You think that, after all I have given you!"

"Given?" he said. "Given? You got as good as you gave. Eh, tell me!" And he gave her a great pinch behind. And then he became sad and said, "But perhaps I have done wrong. Perhaps gone against the Gods. Perhaps you and I do wrong."

"You mean you having that wife back? No good for fuck, her!"

But Paul was not even angry. He spoke half to himself, "He come from the village. My father, my mother, old ghosts them, but he telling me what they say. Seems I broke the order. What order? With the earth, where they bury. Earth, what that mean. *Ogiyan*. Earth. What she? Dirt. But growing corn, yams, fruits, everything. Not liking anyone too big. Not liking me. I break rules. Yes, I break them good. People stand in my way; they got to go. I don't care."

"You win, Paul," she said, "always you winning." But, she thought far down, could he truly win against – them? Oh, not to think that, her job to make him strong!

He hardly heard, but went on: "Maybe I get too like elephant. So what? Why must I get different because old earth, she tell me? How can I go back? Can I live in a village? Can I do without money?"

He had been talking louder and louder, walking up and down, sometimes picking up and handling some bright and valuable thing. Over the years he had been to all sorts of stores, English and Indian, buying what took his fancy. There was one old cannon he had; he wished now he could load it. There were old weapons, spears, bows, but also his new American gun, the neat little gun like in the movies, bound to hit. He had never tried it, only knew to load it, but these guns fired from near, a man couldn't miss.

Some of his friends came round that evening, asking would he go out with them. It was not often he turned his back on a party, but this time he said he must wait in for a phone call, important. "Big deal?" they asked, and clapped him on the back. They were proud of him. But they had not come from his village, not from any village. The earth had lost hold of them. Or almost. Yet if they had been from his village, could he have told them about the old man from the shrine and was it possible they might have stayed with him, might have advised him? Who could advise him now? Not, certainly those foreign advisers who knew how to make money but who would sometimes talk, tediously, of the needs of his country. Why? He was his own country.

After his friends left he went round locking and barring doors, bolting windows, while she followed, anxious but trying to make light of it. He looked at the two cars in the compound, especially the Mercedes-Benz with the tiger upholstery. He had so loved it! But now? The driver slept outside. Could he be trusted? Could anyone be? He had never felt so unsure. There was barb-wire along the top of the brick wall, but – was it enough? Enough for what? That was something he did not know. The steward lived in the compound with his family; he was surely a loyal one. His pay had always been good, better than others gave, besides, all those pickings. He knew! "Come to me if anyone knocks or shouts," he said. "Be sure not to open. I am in danger, you don't want to lose your master."

The steward looked at him gravely, "I understand, Master. But should we not call the police to guard? Tell them Master's enemies prowl and prowl."

"You should do that," the girl said, "Paul – you are well known, you are a big man, a pillar of the city. Why should the police not help you?" But he could not bring himself to telephone, he could not explain. Someone might laugh. Then everything would shatter and whatever it was could rush in.

She cooked him a nice supper, hot the way he liked it. Time he stopped being afraid. She tried to think city-fashion: that old no-good, trying it on! But could he hear her, way off in the shrine? Oh, maybe she should go, find some other kind of protection, get out from under this curse – in case – Paul spoke to her in a breathy whisper, but she took care to answer good and ordinary. Yes, she would go out into the compound after supper, see that the big gate was still barred; then she would lock the house doors, see to the catches on all the windows, in case that old shrine had made him forget one. She put on a record, so that she could hear it, give herself a light step. He was tapping nicely to the record when he heard her scream. Out of the window he saw her, on the ground in the compound beside the cars. He had half a mind to leave her, shut and lock the door on her, let her scream, but instead he grabbed the little gun, loaded it, hurried over. "You hurt?" he said and pulled at her to get her up.

"No," she said, "no, but there, there, on top of the wall, high up!"

"What?" he said, shaking her, "what?"

"A mask!" she half screamed, "Oh why I have to see that! Why!"

He looked. There was nothing. "Moonlight," he said, "Just moonlight on leaves. Silly girl, get up!" He was on one knee beside her, made him feel better, feel big, helping her.

But she pulled at him, then screamed again, "Look!" And there it was, moving jerkily, a black and white appearance, a thing of slits and ridges and holes, a beak looking over the wall. It was what he had half expected when the old man from the shrine said that the earth was angry and unless he did certain things the anger would be passed on to those who must make it plain. But he had not believed. Not by day light. Not here in the city. It was only a long way off, in the village, that the *Ekpo* men happened.

Another mask – but they must have men behind them, they must! And the barb-wire – but could it stop a mask? Kill, then! He fired, but she was pulling at his arm and the little gun did not work for him like guns in the movies work

119

for their masters. There was a crash, but not over the wall. What he had hit was his beautiful car, the Mercedes-Benz, and there was glass everywhere.

That was the first thing the steward saw when he ran out, bravely, into the compound, only held back a minute or two by his wife and indeed by his own great fear, the first thing before he saw the body of his master with the peculiar cuts on its face – but the police when they came at last said they could have been made by the glass. Already insects had come busily to the edge of the crawling blood from the big hole where the life had gone out. And the long-playing record was still dancing on.

Yes, she had tried to telephone at once, but the police do not always answer quickly. Yes, she had grabbed her clothes and yes, a few small trinkets he had given her, yes, maybe costly, but how was she to know? Out of the window she had seen the masks come down and gather. Like crows. What more could she have done? And they had swept away over the wall, over the barb-wire, and there was suddenly nothing. And the beautiful tiger car she had ridden in so softly, smashed, smashed.

To Deal with Witches

The Party Secretary was talking to his immediate comrade Superior over the telephone. He imagined the Superior's office with shaded electric lights and big chairs, a rug, picture calendars and a big fridge full of cold drinks, across one end the big desk with papers arranged by the typing girl in neat piles, the telephone with no bits broken. Perhaps cleaned every day. The Party Secretary was explaining, telling about the last meeting of the committee, "It is bad here. We do not know what to do. The people, they are not coming to meetings. They are not paying their subscriptions. I tell you, I cannot find rent for this office. Maybe the Chairman pays? Maybe. The people not. Everyone is afraid. They do not trust one another. They look sideways."

The voice from the far end said coldly, "I am hoping they trust you still."

"Oh yes, yes!" said the Party Secretary hastily. "I have seen many – secretly. Oh, very many!"

"So what is it? What goes on?"

The Party Secretary hesitated, partly because he did not quite know how to explain in English. Yet, he thought, if I can say it in English, perhaps it will become clear what should be done. "Is difficult – " he began.

The voice came through from that so beautiful far-off desk. "Come, Mr. Simoko, you must know. If not, you are not fit to be Party Secretary."

"Well then, it is like this," said Party comrade Simoko, "there are too many witches – sorcerers – bad people. I do my best. But they are always coming. Crawling in empty houses. First one, then two, then many. There are illnesses, fears, deaths. Perhaps small babies eaten. We cannot tell. Bad spirits hang in the old trees. It is also said – but I have not seen – there is dancing."

"What do you mean – dancing?"

"Women," said Mr. Simoko awkwardly. "No clothes. Not decent. No skirts. Old ladies – witch ladies. That is a big fright."

"You must deal with it," said the other voice. "Call your committee again. They will come, yes? Say it is Party orders. Get in a good doctor, a witch-finder. One who is known to catch witches and destroy bad spirits. Pay out of Party funds."

"Well," said Mr. Simoko, "I will try. Will try my best. Only paying if witches are found. Yes. One Zambia," he added hopefully.

"One Zambia, one nation," the superior voice said. "See to it."

Mr. Simoko put down the telephone, thinking that, unless someone fixed the bracket, it would fall off again, perhaps break some important bit that would stop it talking. But there was no money. People were not interested in politics. They did not understand that an office costs money. Even a little office like this with no desk, only a table with drawers. He must try to get a doctor, a witch-finder, to cure the badness that was eating his people and also his Party. He went home gloomily to consider it all. His wife had cooked a stew. It seemed to be the same stew that she always cooked. Sometimes he read aloud to her from the papers about new, tasty dishes. But she told him she could not get this or that at the market, it was out of season or too expensive. He had given her more money once or twice; it made no difference. She did not bother, did not think about his needs. Better perhaps to spend the money on drink; that helped his sadness.

They had two children, a boy and girl. They were at school, but he did not think they were very clever, not unless he had been drinking. The boy had sore eyes and the ointment from the chemist which had cost plenty did him no good. He often woke up crying; perhaps bad spirits attacked him in his dreams. Perhaps it was the witches.

There had been constant small troubles and illnesses since the witches, the men and women with the bad spirits, had come into the town, settling like flies. Most were in the shanty township at the back of the main road, an easy place for witchcraft or anything else to start. But the infection came through so that nobody felt safe, not in their homes or shopping or in the bars or in the Bank building itself. Not even, thought Mr. Simoko, in the Party office. There had been accidents, a child scalded by an over-turned cooking pot, a lorry going out of control and running into a group of people. Bad, that. There had been a fire at one of the primary schools and at the secondary school a teacher had gone mad. Some of the witches pretended to make money; one shopkeeper had complained but they had threatened him with evil happenings. Although it had been Government inspected, a belt had broken in the engineering works and two men badly hurt. There were altogether too many snakes and rats.

Mr. Simoko was tired hearing of these things all the time, and about the naked dancing which had so upset everyone, since good people certainly love to dance, but like Christians and humanists in their best clothes, or in well-known disguises, but never entirely naked, flapping and dangling themselves. Even small children hid small parts of themselves and their ancestors had always kept the bounds of

123

modesty. But the worst was that nobody was sure who were the witches nor could they by daylight recognise any of the naked dancers as any of their neighbours, because nobody cared to look them in the face. So when there was trouble, no woman would hurry to help her neighbour and men spoke carefully to one another. And every week it was getting worse.

Mr. Simoko found it was not at all easy to find a competent witch-finder, or any kind of doctor whom he could trust to take on this cleaning up job. One thing certain was that the witches came from outside, perhaps from the far ends of the country, since word of a gathering nastiness, a kind of running ulcer on the fair face of Zambia, would spread just as the good word of humanism spread, or at least Mr. Simoko hoped that it spread. Several doctors applied and the first thing they asked was how much money would be given: when Mr. Simoko said that this depended on results some professed themselves insulted. At last one came who was well recommended; he listened to what had been happening and gave Mr. Simoko new ointment for his son's eye, which, he said, had been made from certain herbs as well as the eyes of owls which, it was well known, had specially sharp sight.

So, after Mr. Simoko had consulted his Chairman, although he never thought much of his Chairman's powers of judgment, it was decided to employ this man, who thereupon called on his spirits to fight the spirits of the witches. He threw the usual bones of divination, to guide him to the place where he must fight the powers of witchcraft and tell him which evils he must prepare for. Mr. Simoko gathered some six or eight Party men, all armed. When the doctor had worked himself into a state of mind in which he could recognise the witches, he gave them all small parcels of medicine, wrapped in pieces of hide, to protect them. But one of them, Mr. Kibonde, a youngish man who was already not only a lawyer who had spent two years overseas, but also a poet, refused to take the protective medicine; he said it was against his principles.

Mr. Simoko who was wearing his in the pocket of his shirt, was worried because Kibonde was a man of whom he thought highly and whose opinion he asked when he was puzzled and uncertain about the humanist view point, as he often was. He knew that Kibonde had advised and appeared in Court for quite poor people who had been unjustly treated, because, he said, that was what humanism was about, and often he had taken no money at all. Or again, when the richer people came to him to find out ways round their tax problems, he would only give it if it came strictly within the law. Thus, Kibonde was not rich, but he made poems both in English and, more beautifully, in the spoken language of ordinary people; the English poems were printed in newspapers, but the others were listened to and remembered. So Mr. Simoko begged him to take protection against the malice and hidden traps of the witches. But it was no use.

They all followed the doctor round through the back parts of the town where Mr. Simoko thought the witchcraft was thickest. Here there were no buildings to be proud of, no large signs in English, not even walls or railings. People had just come in and made small houses out of anything they could find: tin boxes beaten out, cardboard, sticks. There were no drains, but at least there was water in the standpipes and it should have been pleasant enough for the women who came with pails and jugs. But they were not stopping under the shade trees to gossip and laugh: not now. The Party crowd followed the doctor round and soon he threw himself onto the hard ground in front of a hut and scrabbled with his hands and at last pulled something out which Mr. Simoko did not like to look at. A woman came running out of the house and went into a fit. "Confess, confess!" shouted the doctor while two of the party held her tight. The doctor blew his medicines all over her face; in a while, after flapping and screaming, she seemed to go blank and answered easily. Yes, she had danced, opening naked legs, yes, her spirits had ridden her and made her do this and that to her neighbours. But she had not chosen to be a witch and at once she named another woman who had brought her in and when she gave the name there was shouting and agreement from all the people who had gathered round. "This one will do no more harm," said the doctor and he put the thing which he had found, wrapped in newspaper after it had been treated with his medicine powder, into a black plastic bag which he was carrying. The woman sat on the ground holding her head and moaning. "Poor thing," said Kibonde.

They went on to the one who had been named and the witch-finder duly pulled a thing of great nastiness out of the thatch above her door. But she was more difficult, screamed at them, said it was all lies, the thing had been put there by some enemy. The doctor tried the powder, but she only sneezed; he sang magic words at her, and exhorted her to tell the truth but instead of listening she only shouted at him and was joined by a large and strong man who said he was her husband and would take them to Court if they slandered her any more. Unaccountably the people who seemed to have agreed that the woman was a witch had all melted away. It was then that Mr. Simoko began to suspect that his doctor was not as confident and successful as he had made out.

Certainly he found a few more the next day after he had eaten and slept and accepted a donation from Party funds. Some confessed more or less, others said no; while it was going on the neighbours sneaked up or came rushing, mostly pleased, sometimes angry. There was one empty hut whose owner had run. But it did not appear that this doctor could get what was so desperately needed: a mass movement by the witches, men and women alike, to confession, promise of reform, perhaps begging the bystanders to beat the evil spirits out of them, and of course willingness to help the Party and be instructed in the cause of Zambian humanism, even if they did not understand it. If only he could have that to report to Headquarters! But he must certainly find another doctor who would not tire so easily. The other Party men were disappointed. They had wanted some action on behalf of the Party and though they had thumped one or two male witches on the second and third day, but not enough to break bones, it was not what they really wanted. Yet they did not know what they wanted, except for Kibonde who was making a poem about the ending of trouble and flowers coming out everywhere. That was all very fine, but none of it would happen unless the witches were all rooted out and everyone joined together and thanked the Party for what had been done.

This doctor said he would come back when he had done certain things to refresh himself and his spirits. But he did not come back, and the nurse at the Clinic came over angrily to tell Mr. Simoko that there was an outbreak of measles at one of the schools and the drugs she had asked for had not come through and furthermore there was a snake under the roof of the clinic and what was he going to do about it? So clearly things were not yet going right, and another doctor must be found or the witches would lie back and laugh at him and the Party.

Another Doctor came who sounded as though he might have the necessary powers; he had a special Bible which had been treated so that it would give sure signs of a witch. "For instance," he said, "any sincere person can try this for himself." And he told Mr. Simoko to open it at random and lay his finger over a few words. If he was truly anxious to rid the town of witches and to keep his promises, including generous payment for the work to be done, then a sign would be given. Mr. Simoko held the magic Bible very cautiously, not wanting to open it too wide, while the doctor said a prayer, then shut his eyes and opened it. The words his finger covered were:—

'And, behold, there came an old man from his work out of

the field at even, which was also of Mount Ephraim; and
he sojourned in Gibeah: but the men of the place were
Benjamites.'

"That will mean the chief witch is an old man," said the
doctor, "perhaps the oldest in the place. He will have strong
spirits." The doctor shook his head, "These old men!
Elephant with broken tusk, most dangerous. He will have
made many sacrifices. Come from outside, bad, powerful,
not Christian like me. But we shall find him."

So this doctor prepared himself and all went with him, but
not too near. He did not give them parcels of medicine or
mask them in any way, because, he said, this magic Bible
would protect them. From time to time this doctor opened
his magic Bible and read from it in a loud voice; when he did
this the horn that was hanging round his neck jumped about;
it had strong medicines packed into it. Sometimes he would
stop to look about him, smelling. Perhaps he was watching
for a sign and perhaps it might come from the people who
had been suffering and themselves were watching, whether
in fear or hope. It was a hot day and the smells bad. But one
latrine no use for this crowd and that was all there had been
funds for. Maybe ten needed, Mr. Simoko thought, and a
proper drain made. Suddenly the doctor plunged through a
doorway into a hut and pulled out quite an old man, but
decently dressed in shirt and trousers, no witch bags or
hyena tails. "I'm no witch," he shouted, and then to Mr.
Simoko, "Was it not I myself who was in the front applauding
your speech and in the end put some nice money into the
collection? More than I should have done for I am not rich,
no! But I liked your words." And then he stood at attention
like a policeman and shouted "One Zambia!"

This made it all very difficult. One of the escort pulled at
Mr. Simoko and whispered, "Is correct. That old man, he
was at the meeting," and then he shouted, "Does anyone
accuse him?" One woman said, "My hens they stop laying."
But she did not say it very firmly and nobody else spoke.

Another woman said, "This is not the bad one – go further." There were hands pointing. The escort looked at one another, then one of them went over and shook hands with the old man saying "One Zambia comrade." But the doctor was angry. In the end he did less well that the first one and complained of attacks from the bad spirits which were giving him terrible belly-aches. And still there was no sign of the great clearing up and confessions that were so necessary for the Party.

For a while Mr. Simoko did nothing, though his friend Kibonde tried to cheer him up. Mr. Simoko began to get more and more tired of his wife and his son blinking away with those ugly sore eyes that got no better in spite of the owl ointment. It was in the end Kibonde who found another doctor. She was from the west, Malilo, daughter of Hamatete. She had been educated, but in her last year at secondary school when her teachers had begun to speak of University, she started to have dreams which all pointed one way. She struggled against this, because it was not certain whether they were the work of good spirits or bad. Her mother was dead and Malilo went to her grave with offerings and tears and some fear; in the dreams that followed her mother spoke to her, saying she must not be afraid, but must accept that she had been chosen to cast out bad spirits. It was allowed for her mother's shade to help, but she must go through certain rites which might go against what she had learnt at school.

Malilo had not wanted to do this; she was frightened, she wanted to learn other kinds of things, to be a stenographer or an airline hostess or even a nurse. But no, the spirits needed her. More than once she was tempted to become a witch herself. Power grew in her. She began to be able to heal; her hands could do things to people, making them feel one way or the other. Sometimes this feeling of power made her want to punish people, but she struggled with herself, knowing that this would put her feet on a bad path. People came to her for love charms and at first she gave them, but once this turned into a disaster and ended with a man's wife hanging herself. After that she stopped altogether having dealings with these charms.

About then Malilo began to know that she could recognise those, like herself, with power, but with bad power. She set herself now only to heal and help. She had courage; she went to those she could feel were witches and begged them not to harm but only to heal. Just once or twice this worked well; they were persuaded. They became healers. But most saw their living go if they did not frighten people and then make them pay for charms or for being told who had injured them, so they were angry with Malilo. But now she herself began to know who was likely to have done an injury; it was terrible for her to know. For a time the world seemed to be full of badness; must she alone deal with it all? Once in a small village she saw very clearly someone with bad powers and told the Chief of the village. But that was the worst thing that ever came to her, for the Chief had the woman seized and brought to him, then beaten and branded with hot irons and afterwards, screaming all the time, turned over to his people who did further things to her, although Malilo pleaded that the bad spirits had been destroyed and no more should be done. For many nights after that the woman's screaming went on in her dreams. So now she worked mostly in secret and the only punishment she allowed, since blood must be shed to kill the bad spirits, was by small cuts on the cheeks and chest which she made herself with a razor which she had dedicated to her mother.

Malilo was a Party member, since she had decided that the Party tried to help poor people and children, but she did not often go to meetings. It hurt her to feel the jealousies and lies and anger that so often came up in them. Her father had found for her a prosperous, sensible husband, but she said no. She did not think she could be a good wife. Other things would stand in the way. But she was not an ugly girl; she had fine eyes and a good figure which is what men mostly want. Indeed it seemed to her that she had yielded once or twice to men, but when she was in the full tide of her dreams and her healing, she was often not certain about the world outside. If later on, her spirits told her she could marry, then it would be time enough. Kibonde had seen her at work in a village infected with witchcraft; he had seen her cutting the witches with the razor while they confessed and promised, and while she did it, she herself was weeping. He made a poem about this in which Malilo was a rain cloud. And now he spoke about her to Mr. Simoko.

"Get her, get her!" said Mr. Simoko, "but I hope she will not ask for too much money. There is little left and I have nowhere to keep my papers in the office!" Things were not going well for him. The girl had sore eyes now and both of them cried at night when Mr. Simoko wanted to sleep. And that morning a letter had come from his youngest uncle, asking for a loan till after harvest – and was he likely to pay then! No doubt that was nothing to do with the witches, but somehow things were heaping up. He would so much have liked to have a cheerful, thriving town so that he could one day ask for a Minister to come down and give a speech and perhaps open something.

So in a day or two Kibonde came into the office and said this woman was waiting at the station. Those who had come before had all marched straight and boastingly into the office and looked round, as though, Mr. Simoko thought, they were looking for the cash drawer. Perhaps she was, after all, a modest woman? – in spite of being a doctor. But how could one tell? They went down to the station which was quite small because there were few trains. "There she is," said Kibonde and there, sure enough, was a woman sitting on the ground in the shade of the big jacaranda tree. She stayed very quiet, not moving while they walked towards her over the cinders of the platform. There were jacaranda flowers that had dropped here and there on her head scarf or

132

her bare arms. She had a cardboard suit case with a strap round it and a big bundle done up in a cloth from the western region. She looked up at Mr. Simoko and he fell in love with her, at once and altogether, like falling into a deep river.

She greeted them in a voice that had a touch of the Lozi accent. It was a quiet voice, a suitable voice for a woman, but it had authority. Kibonde said, "Here is the Party Secretary, Mr. Simoko."

She looked hard at Mr. Simoko and said, "I must speak with you. Let us sit."

Mr. Simoko's heart gave a great jump. Could it possibly be that the same thing had happened, that this woman had seen the same light that he had? There was a bench under the tree, but she still sat on the ground like any country woman; he sat down beside her, as close as he dared. He wished Kibonde would go away, but Kibonde sat on the bench with a notebook and pencil.

Malilo said yes, she was indeed a doctor, she could tell who were in the power of bad spirits and were led or forced into becoming witches. Her own spirits, especially the shade of her mother, told her this. She had been chosen to cast out evil. Why? She did not know, and it was tiring. Often she was sad. It was here that Mr. Simoko longed to hold her hand. "I too have been sad," he said and moved a little inch closer to her, though it was uncomfortable on the cinders. She however did not move at all. She said to Mr. Simoko, "Tell me about the part of the town where the witches are. Our friend Kibonde says that they are poor people who have come in from the country, mostly. What have you and the Party done for them?"

This was a strange question from a witch-finder. For a moment Mr. Simoko could not think of an answer. Was she blaming him? He gave up hope that she loved him, as for a moment he had dared to think. He began hastily to tell her about the clinic, with inoculations and family planning. There was a new primary school planned, but the Ministry had said nothing yet. Trees? She told him that certain trees, not the dark old trees, baobabs and such, but especially young fruit trees, nourished good spirits; perhaps he could get some trees and every family should plant one. This would be done, he said, yes, yes!

"People who make things are less troubled," said Malilo, "you could start a small co-operative." He agreed again, but found it a strange thing for a witch-finder to say to him. "And you yourself, Mr. Party Secretary, you are not very happy." She said this in just the same way that she had said everything else. Could she mean what he wished she could mean? No, no, take nothing for granted. He could not look in her eyes. Instead he looked at her ears. She had very small earrings, the kind a child might have. Perhaps they were the same her parents had given when she was only a little girl. A little loved girl.

In a while he answered her question about himself. Was he happy? "No. But now, I think, yes."

"You could be healed," she said broodingly, and for a moment he thought of a gift of earrings, of necklaces, of bracelets. But where was the money? And might she not push them away? He did not know. "Come!" she said and "Come Kibonde, this is not time for making poems. We must work!" And in one movement she was up and onto her feet. Kibonde took her suitcase. Mr. Simoko made to take her bundle, but she held up her hand. "Now," she said, throwing back her head, "it is there!" And she pointed in the direction where indeed the witch-ridden township lay.

They moved in, on one of the trodden paths between the huts. She carried the bundle on her head as any ordinary woman would have done. Nothing happened, not for a time. Then suddenly everything happened. She had looked for nothing in the ground or under the thatch, had cast no spell nor thrown any powders or charms, nothing which could have been expected. She did not throw the objects of divination, nor had she given any protection to Mr. Simoko or Kibonde or any of the Party people who had followed cautiously. Only she had stopped several times and stood silently, as if listening to something inward. After the first few minutes people had come creeping and gathering and following as though they were aware of something.

She sat down on an old box and waited. Then, out of the crowd, one person after another came, shivering, weeping, and knelt in front of her. Although it was clear that these were the witches, nobody tried to hurt them or even touch them. She spoke to them one after another, sometimes also touching them. Out of the bundle that she had carried on her head she took the razor. After she had spoken with each of them she cut them and blood mingled with tears poured down their faces and down the bony chests of the men or the tops of the breasts, scraggy or plump, of the women. She also gave them a small, bitter drink from a bottle she had in the bundle and sometimes she tied things onto them. All round her there grew a dreadful heap of the objects of sorcery which now had been thrown away. It took a long time and nobody had eaten. Suddenly Malilo said, "No more, no more!" There were witches clinging to her, some pleading, some wide-eyed with fear; a few more were edging towards her through the crowd. "I will come back," she said to them, almost as a mother might have. "Wait for me. Do not move. Do not hurt."

She rose to her feet shivering and, one at each side, Kibonde and Mr. Simoko supported her. It was apparent that her own fingers, too, had been cut by the edge of the razor, for the blood still oozed out of them, though she did not seem to notice. "She must eat," said Kibonde, anxiously, "but where?"

"At my home," said Mr. Simoko, "She can be quiet there. But you, Kibonde, my friend, you must take out my wife – she will disturb – ask questions – Get her away for an hour, two hours! While this woman of God eats and sleeps."

So that was the way it was left. They walked with her to

Mr. Simoko's house and a basin of cold water was brought, so that she could wash off the blood. She seemed to have a special cloth for this, sweet-smelling. She ate an orange, slowly, then a banana, would not take more. But her eyelids were fluttering with tiredness. "She must sleep," said Kibonde anxiously, "Let her sleep on your bed and I will take out the lady of the house."

Now it must be said that the poet Kibonde had a bicycle. He took Mrs. Simoko off on the carrier of the bicycle and went in the direction of the forest. She was cross when she left the house and used bitter language, needing to be sweet-talked by Kibonde before she would get onto the carrier. But when she came back it appeared that she was entirely cheerful and smiling.

But Malilo the daughter of Hamatete slept and slept. Mr. Simoko was anxious. She had done so well; could she possibly go on with it? Had she so much power that she could deal with all the witches and sorcerers, even the strongest? He pulled up a chair and sat watching her asleep and slowly the lines of strength and tension faded from round her eyes and mouth and she became soft to look at. And she was asleep in the large brass-ended bed of Mr. Simoko. So it came about that slowly, slowly, and deep in love, Mr. Simoko took off, first his shoes and then his trousers and shirt. Could he perhaps lie where he could touch Malilo? Gently, with no disturbance. Only to touch.

So he too lay down on the bed and there was no creaking or rustling. But he seemed to be coming nearer so that first his fingers and then other parts of him began to touch Malilo, and he felt goodness streaming out into him. He put his face close to hers and her breath came very slowly and her eyes were closed. When his lips touched her eyelids it appeared that she did not feel them, so deep down she was. His toes approached, touched her instep. His hands went down towards them. The edge of her skirt was loose, not, as he had feared, caught under her. It was light in his hand. He pressed between her thighs, gently, and, as gently, they opened, gave him passage. He wished he had no weight, wished he were a butterfly settling on the soft, the quivering petals of a flower. But still she slept and, in her sleep, smiled. She had a buttoned bodice, but he slid one hand cleverly up to fondle, to feel the tips press into his palm. So he went in and she, it seemed, came entirely in tune with him as he murmured her name over and over with light kisses on her neck and her ears with their small, valueless earrings.

For a moment she opened her eyes and in those dark pools he drowned again. She seemed to have no surprise to find him there, only her lips quivered and where he had been there was warmth and throbbing and comfort. Had it been true? He looked at her. He looked at himself. Yes, this wonderful thing had truly happened and he would never be the same again. He would be a better man. Nobody would understand. Only perhaps Kibonde. But how could he ever speak of it? Quietly, quietly, he dressed again and pulled her skirt down, over her so beautiful soft parts, taking one last, long look at them, and at last covering almost to her ankles. He tiptoed down to look at the clock, for his own watch was not going well.

When he came back she suddenly sat up and said, "I am a little hungry and I must go back soon."

"Everything in my house is yours," he said. But all the same he could not find much. Still, he made a sandwich with bread and butter and fried her an egg. He did not like the look of the cold stew or the soggy rice. She ate like a hungry child and seemed not to know that anything had passed except sleep since she had dealt with the witches. "It is tiring to do that" she said, "More tiring than anything in the world, but now I have stopped being tired. I have had good dreams. I shall go back and find the last of the witches for you. If I can do this, then do it I will."

"For me," said the Party Secretary, hoping that she might say some sweet thing. For surely she must have been aware of his part in her good dreams. "For Zambia" she said.

Mr. Kibonde came back and the two women greeted one another as two old friends might have done. The children came in from school and their eyes seemed better and Mr. Simoko thought that his own two were nice children; he liked the way they moved and spoke. He had been afraid that his wife would be sulky, not even polite to the woman of God. But no, all was peace and pleasantness. Perhaps I have misjudged that wife of mine, thought Mr. Simoko, perhaps if I could make her happy as it seems I have made the other happy, things might get better. And indeed this became true, because on their way back from the forest, which had so many beautiful thick obscuring bushes, the wife had asked Kibonde to stop at a certain market stall. She knew she could get there those two or three things which can make a stew really good, but which she had not bothered about before since it did not seem worth while. But the next day there was a stew which was too nice altogether, and her husband complimented her and made nice jokes, and it became as if they were just married.

But before that, Malilo daughter of Hamatete with Kibonde and Mr. Simoko and many of the Party – for word had spread – went back to that same place in the township where they had been before. By now it was beginning to be dusk, but people had brought candles and small lanterns and made a circle round her. And at the back of the circle the witches and sorcerers were waiting to confess and be healed of their evil spirits which were now paining them, and become one with their neighbours. At midnight she stopped for a while and seemed to pray, for she became very still and her lips moved. Neither Mr. Simoko nor his friend Kibonde spoke, but both stood guard beside her until she was ready. They knew that she needed to gather all her power, since it is at midnight that evil works its will. But when that danger was past it all began again.

Before it was over dawn was beginning and came quickly.

Her fingers were bleeding again, but she seemed not to notice. She looked round and asked for torn newspapers, sticks, branches, pieces of old thatch. They made a fire and she heaped onto it the objects of sorcery and the witch clothing, the tails of animals and the masks, as also the ointment which they had used when they danced naked. The flames licked up round them and that thing was ended.

When the fire had finished its work many people came to thank her. It appeared that some of the witches had moved away entirely. Their houses were burnt and the ashes from the destroying fire added to their own ashes. "After this," said Malilo, "You will plant small trees. Nobody must make a house where one of theirs was."

"And now," said Kibonde, "the Party will pay you."

"Very well," she said, and then "You will have no more trouble."

Mr. Simoko unlocked the cash drawer and took out the Party money. If only he had not given any to those useless ones! There was not very much. He made a heap of kwacha notes and a small heap of two kwachas and wished he knew of a magic to turn the ones into tens. Malilo looked on with no great eagerness, only as a sensible and trusting girl might do. When he had made the heaps tidy she picked them up and halved both of them. She pushed her piles over and said "This is for the Party. You could buy small trees. Fruit trees would be good, do you think?"

Mr. Simoko was too surprised to be able to speak properly. He only muttered, "Yes, yes, we will do what you say."

She looked at him sweetly and said "Perhaps you should plant a tree by your own home. It will bring good spirits." And then she looked from Mr. Simoko to Kibonde. "And you will make for me a poem? Yes, I would like that so much. And now, I think there is a train back."